To has gone Steve.

'Short Circuit' and other Geek Stories

Love,
Ken

'Short Circuit' and other Geek Stories

Kenna McKinnon

Copyright (C) 2016 Kenna McKinnon
Layout Copyright (C) 2016 Creativia

Published 2016 by Creativia
Paperback design by Creativia (www.creativia.org)
ISBN: 978-1532918780
Cover art by http://www.thecovercollection.com/
This book is a work of fiction. Names, characters, places, and incidents are the product of the author's imagination or are used fictitiously. Any resemblance to actual events, locales, or persons, living or dead, is purely coincidental. All rights reserved. No part of this book may be reproduced or transmitted in any form or by any means, electronic or mechanical, including photocopying, recording, or by any information storage and retrieval system, without the author's permission.

For my son Steven Robert Wild
April 8, 1968 – September 21, 2012
You shine brightly in our memory

Contents

The Sea and His Guitar	1
A Classic Meeting	3
A Cowboy in Maidenhead	4
Knock, Knock the Robots Are Here	17
Short Circuit	22
The Geese	26
The Ham Sandwich	34
The Minotaur	36
Grandmother's Story	39
How They Met	42
Indeterminate Time in Hell	43
Perversion	45

The Devil and His Imps, Indeterminate Time	47
The Preacher in Osoyoos	51
The End	55
Unclean	60
Awful Waffles	62
Cyclops	66
Waiting for Nikolai	68
Long Walk To Gadara	70
Matters about Monty	79
Ghoul Bite, Sweet Prince	81
It's the Bees' Knees	84
It's The Bees' Knees 2	87
It's The Bees' Knees 3	89
It's The Bees' Knees 4	91
Apocalypse	94
Wild Honey	96
Music Of The Spheres	102
About The Author	104

The Sea and His Guitar

The pain was electric music in his gut, placated by Morphine. He slept until the friend woke him.

"Your son... the boy you never knew as an adult, what became of him? Your mother's grandson."

"I met him at Brewster's a few days ago. He didn't recognize me. I explained I couldn't help it, the absences, the silence, they were imposed on me by his family."

"He knows that?"

"I don't know. My son plays guitar, too. Electric. My mother bought him his first guitar."

"Too cool."

"The black acoustic and the Godin are mine."

"You have three amps and one is real nice, a vintage 1960s Vox you got from Craig's List."

"No, I got it from Kijiji. I live in Alberta, Kijiji's big here. I took the bus to the guy's place, paid him cash on the spot."

"Nice Vox."

"I see the posters, can peek out the window at the street and the sun when the drapes are open, like now."

"You're miles from the ocean but I see your favorite ocean videos on Netflix, Van Gogh and the Scream on your living room wall."

"Yes, I like the sea and the Scream. I like the stars. My sister lives in Vancouver. We went whale watching a couple of times; took a lot of great photos, and saw the Aquarium. The jellyfish were my favorites, beautiful colors and shapes."

"Did you want to go back some day? Live there?"

"Too much on the fault line and too far from home. I'm a homebody."

"Too bad. The sea is our mistress."

"Yes. Music is our mistress, too. The stars and the Scream."

The cream-colored Vox amp stood in the corner, unused by the grandson after his father surrounded himself with the ocean; the wild dark sea and the music, dived into the night of the underworld and swam to the other side of the Universe where the stars blazed and the Scream was left behind.

"I have my memories," the father's son said and declined a recent photograph of the handsome young man in his forties, face illuminated and eyes wise and humorous.

We all have our memories, the guitar still sang—his black acoustic instrument in particular sang in the hands of the friend, who moderated the dead man's celebration of life when the sea and the Light claimed him again, back to the bosom of Unconsciousness and no more pain.

A Classic Meeting

She was twenty-nine that year, in September of 1974, and early for her first class of the morning. She sat in the front row, toward the right, in which direction the professor leaned coming through the door.

"A woman is like a rose," the professor said, ducking her head at the podium and reading from a Greek work in translation.

Intermittent joy — intermittent despair — ensued for the next thirty-nine years. Intervening husbands, children, wars, and politics. The student valued thought; the professor valued a career in academics. She who valued thought became enmeshed in her feelings. She who valued feelings was ensnared by a profession that valued thought.

Aphrodite (Venus) and Athena ran a footrace to win a golden apple from handsome Paris. Aphrodite won.

There is no escape from Aphrodite, the goddess of love, not even with Athena, who sprang wise from the brow of her father, Zeus.

Both lovely and kind women. The professor and the student.

They each had handsome sons and beautiful daughters. The jewels in their crown of life.

The jewels, as they both aged, and the apple passed to other hands.

A Cowboy in Maidenhead

Under the tilt of his cowboy hat, Ross Graham's Afro-Canadian face was black and rugged. Grey stubble tickled Cynthia's chin as he bent to kiss her cheek. The white apron she wore around her waist made her appear shorter and rounder than usual. Ross liked that. Don't talk to Ross about diets and weight loss, weight lifting and running.

"Just enjoy your meals, woman, and if you come back to Alberta, Canada with me, I'll cook you the juiciest Angus beefsteak you've ever tasted from the barbecue. And Canadian Club whisky with ice."

"Better than the Beefeaters?" Cynthia meant the gin.

"Better than gin and lime." Ross poured them drinks frequently during that first week and he smoked Cuban cigars in the house, with the windows open.

"Better than cocaine," he said.

"Oh, Ross." Cynthia wrung her hands and twittered. "How you talk. Crikey."

The Afro-Canadian cowboy wore faded blue jeans with a huge round nickel belt buckle fastened to one side, beneath his belly. There was a pack of chewing gum in his back pocket. When in Cynthia's house, he took off his boots. The boots were sweat-stained and tooled, with one-inch heels, and so snug that he used a long shoe horn to remove them.

Cynthia didn't believe his droll stories about his ancestors tending cattle in the Hebrides before the Highland Clearances, before his great grandparents had immigrated to Canada. She wasn't daft. She knew about Alberta, Montana and the U.S. His home in Canada was the same to her as Montana or the Hebrides. A cowboy was a cowboy.

What was he doing here in England? In Berkshire? In Maidenhead?

Cynthia had never met a character like the dark man in plaid shirt and boots. Cynthia lived in a council house in Maidenhead, part of the Royal Borough of Windsor and Maidenhead. Ross Graham had rented a black lorry at Heathrow Airport and set out for the Royal Borough. He ended up at a pub in Maidenhead where old Tom Squire directed him to Cynthia's B&B. They got along right away and she offered him room and board for the week.

"Where's this Prince of Wales?" Ross asked Cynthia the day after he had settled into his new digs. "I came all the way to London to meet the guy who's going to be king." They were sitting on a pink satin settee in her living room. She was working on a MENSA booklet.

"You mean Prince Charles?"

"Yes. The guy who likes trees and old buildings. Charles, Prince of Wales." Ross took a pencil and added a flourish to the equation with which Cynthia struggled. "There. That completes a logarithmic solution to the problem, Cynth."

"Elegant," she said. "That was the only question I didn't get."

The smoke alarm screeched. Steam issued from the stressed pressure cooker in the kitchen.

"Oh, damn." Ross put down the pencil.

"It's going to blow." Cynthia settled deeper into the 19th century settee.

"Probably." Ross grunted and admired his solution.

Cynthia peeked at the answer. "Oh, look, luv. They say we're in the top third. That's ace."

Sustained whistling came from the kitchen and the pot rattled on the old stove. "Yep. It's gonna blow," Ross said. "Never did trust them pressure cookers."

A Cowboy in Maidenhead

"Potatoes, corned beef, swedes everywhere," Cynthia said. "It will be a real mess."

"Rutabagas," Ross said. He selected a Cuban cigar from a wooden box and chewed off the end, then struck a match and lit the cigar. He drew deeply on the stogie. Cynthia opened a window. The smoke alarm continued to shriek. She took out the battery and attempted to rescue the stew. There was a burst of steam from the kitchen, another piercing whistle, and the pot exploded.

Swedes, potatoes, meat and gravy oozed down the yellow walls and ceiling. It was visible even from the next room. Ross took another puff of his cigar. The smoke alarm stuttered and stopped. Cynthia wailed.

Ross drawled, "Ride a cock horse to Banbury Cross to see a fine lady upon a white horse.

Rings on her fingers and bells on her toes, she shall have music…"

"…wherever she goes." Cynthia wiped her hands on her apron and untied the strings from behind her back. "I could have been killed," she said.

"Well, let's go out for a meal, shall we?" The tall Afro-Canadian got up and began to pull on his boots.

"Good idea," Cynthia said. "Just give me a minute." She swiped at a brown viscous blob of meat sliding its way down the wall next to the electric meter. "Your lorry or my car?"

"My truck. Don't like your puny little tin can." Ross contemplated the gravy on the wall. "I'm taking the truck out tomorrow. There's a herd of wild horses in Kent, I heard. I've been meaning to check it out. Came all the way to England to check out the wild horses here and talk to the Prince. Seems to me a fella could make a few thousand pounds taming horseflesh here. Maybe rent a horsebox for transporting them if the truck ain't big enough. I do love wild horses. Not a lot of 'em left at home in Alberta. I hunted them all down near Lethbridge one summer, in a canyon there, magnificent animals, Cynth. I broke a few."

"Broke?" Cynthia adjusted her hair in front of a cracked mirror in the hallway. Ross sucked on the stump of his cigar. Stew began to drip from the kitchen ceiling. He could see it from where they stood chatting.

"That means I tamed them for riding," he explained.

"Oh. Cowboys break horses, milk cows..."

"Cowpokes don't milk cows. We run thousands of head on open ranges, round them up in the fall, sell them at the market for beef. Farmers milk cows, eh." Ross ran his hand over a neat thatch of wiry salt and pepper hair.

Cynthia smiled at him and twisted a strand of his hair between her fingers. "I don't think you're allowed to break these wild horses in Kent. They're protected by conservationists."

"Such as the Prince?" Ross ground out his cigar in a half shell which served as an ashtray by the settee.

"Yes, I suppose so. Well, yes, Charles is interested."

"I want to see the Prince of Wales." Ross scratched the back of his neck. "He's gonna help me cull that herd."

"Cull the herd?" Cynthia brushed a piece of lint from his lapels.

"Take out the feistiest of them. Thin the herd and take the ones I want."

"You'd come all the way back here from Kent with a herd of wild horses in a lorry?"

"Do it all the time at home," the cowboy said.

"How are you going to make money off that?" Cynthia asked.

"Oh, a good piece of broke horseflesh will fetch a tidy sum at the auction."

"Blimey," she said. "That's brill. Is it lots of work?"

Ross laughed. He tipped his hat in the afternoon sun as they left the red brick council house. "No more than shearing sheep," he said. "A well-trained pony can do many things."

"Such as?"

"Oh, horse racing. Sheep or cattle herding. Amusement. Riding. Carousels. Fox hunting? I've heard of that. Don't tell me there's no 'do ye ken John Peel'." Cynthia glanced again at the mess behind them before they left her house.

Ross opened the door of the truck and Cynthia clambered in. She adjusted her hair again, looking in the rearview mirror.

"That's debatable," she said. "Fox hunts anyway. But if you say so."

When they reached the pub, Ross began to draw diagrams and pictograms on a paper napkin.

"This is the herd," he explained. "This is the equation for calculating where they'll be at a given moment of time, their behavior if approached in an infinity of ways—"

Ross ordered a pint of Guinness for himself and gin and lime for Cynthia. A piece of steamed potato was congealed to her shoe. She scraped it off with her other shoe, staring at the bottom of the glass, which magnified the diagrams on the paper napkin. With a few strokes of her own pencil, Cynthia completed the equation. The herd on paper fell out of their universe and disappeared from the napkin. Ross picked it up and shook it with a pink-palmed hand.

"Darn," he said. "So it's true what they say. There's a wormhole."

"Wormhole?" Cynthia asked. "You're a bloody barmy fella."

"Where y'all get language like that? Not from the Prince."

"I know worse than that, luv. But the Prince, he's a real gentleman." Cynthia coughed.

"How would you know that?" Ross scratched the grey stubble on his chin.

"I live ten minutes from Windsor Castle," she replied. "I've seen the Royals going to and fro a number of times."

"In his garden?"

"No. It's not open to the public. Beautiful gardens. I'd like to see them, as well."

"How do I meet him?" Ross's incisor teeth bit at his lower lip.

"Request an audience with the Prince of Wales, I suppose. I don't know," Cynthia said. "Take him to tea. I don't know."

That's what he did. The very next day, Ross and Charles had tea together, the Afro-Canadian cowboy who won the west, and the king in waiting.

It happened because the universe had slipped through a knot in the string theory and a monarch thus could have afternoon tea with a cowboy. It was improbable but possible, like the literary monkeys in another story. Charles thought the appointment had been set a year ago by his Secretary, and Ross thought the English were as informal as his Aunt Mildred. The tea was excellent but served in china cups which didn't fit the cowboy's thick fingers. They exchanged family stories. They discussed disambiguation, string theory and quantum physics. Charles was adamant. They disagreed on the existence of parallel universes but agreed their equations pointed towards a unified theory of gravity, which Einstein hadn't quite had time to figure out.

Charles was, at heart, a conservationist and the horses were to be left alone. No, breaking the horses wouldn't solve the oil crisis, Charles assured Ross. But… "that's why I came to England,", Ross said, and let's ask Cynthia.

No.

Tomorrow the wild ponies in Kent, the lorry ride back to Maidenhead, the rented pastures, then the trouble — but now Cynthia's deep-set blue-green eyes, the velvet ivory skin, and the improbability of this encounter.

The black-faced sheep in Berkshire gave up their wool to the cloth factories. The herd of wild horses gamboled in Kent. Cynthia and Ross decided to ignore the Prince's decision and go to Kent the very next day with the rented truck and a rope. Ross said he would ride a Kentish pony to Banbury Cross… *to see a fine lady upon a white horse.* Elizabeth I the Tudor Virgin Queen who rode a white stallion to Banbury to see a Celtic Cross, as the story goes. "*Whoop whoop,*" yodeled Ross, "Giddee up, Old Paint." The Old World was assaulted by the New. A thoughtful Prince knew enough to check his charges in Kent thereafter. Unfortunately, he was called away that week on business and the younger Royals were otherwise too engaged to care.

The cowboy attracted stares as he ambled down the Old World streets of Maidenhead. His New World won the confrontation until, as had been predicted, equilibrium was re-established.

"While we're talking of the Royals..." Ross changed his shirt after tea with the Prince because he had spilled Crème Brûlée on it. "The first Queen Elizabeth. The Virgin Queen." He winked at Cynthia.

"You're my queen."

"Don't kid yourself, luv," she said.

That night, Ross and Cynthia cleaned the kitchen, her old wood-encased radio turned to a classic station. She asked him if he liked music.

"Yeah," Ross said. "I like music, Cynth."

"What kind of music?" Cynthia asked. "Blues?" She guessed. "That awful moaning musical saw, what was his name—Slim? Isn't that cowboy music?"

"Slim Whitman. My mother's favorite," Ross said. "When I was a boy..." He stuck his chewing gum neatly in a wrapper and put it in a cup on the counter. "When I was just a tadpole," he continued, "we worked on a ranch for the boss man. The boss man was fat, lazy and white. He didn't like African Canadians. One day, my mother hung colored bottles on a big old green ash tree, all sizes, shapes, and colors, and they tinkled so pretty in the wind that day. I was spellbound. Until the boss man came along. He broke all them pretty bottles with his stick, he did. There was glass everywhere. We had to clean it up. I didn't mind for myself, but my mama—all that work. My mama had dreams. She liked music."

"How old were you then, Ross?" Cynthia continued to scrub the kitchen walls. Ross handed her a sponge and leaned against the doorway in his sock feet.

"About nine."

"Anything good ever happened to you growing up with that boss man?" Cynthia wrung out the cloth in the sink and sprayed the ceiling with a biodegradable cleaner. Ross took a cloth and wiped the walls.

"Yeah. I always liked books. One day, when I was eighteen, he called me into his office. He was very frail by then, sick and riddled with diabetes and sores on his legs. He apologized to me for his behavior all those years and offered to send me to law school. He said I was a smart kid, one of the brightest he'd met, and he'd like me to go through university."

"Well, that's very nice. Did you major in cowboy?"

Ross laughed. "I didn't take him up on his offer. Now I wished I had. I hated him by that time."

Cynthia finished rinsing the walls and ceiling. The tiles on the walls shone. "You did the right thing, Ross. But why did he offer, after all that time, if he was as mean as you say he was? Did you ever figure that out?"

"I always thought it was guilt." Ross admired the gleaming walls. He turned, ambled to the living room and sat down.

"I don't think so. He wanted a son?" Cynthia left the kitchen and sat beside Ross on the old green sofa that was next to the settee.

"He had a son. The son hated me too."

"Crikey. Did his son want to go to law school?"

"No. He wanted to party and spend all his father's wealth."

"Wealth? He owned the ranch?

Ross dangled his hands over his knees. "Yeah. But it turned out at the end, after he died many years later and they opened his will, that he didn't have as much as everyone thought. He'd spent most of it on his son's shenanigans and keeping the ranch going. He'd experimented with a new breed of cows a few years before and it didn't work out. Lost a lot of money. We had a few dry years then in southern Alberta, lost all the crop, had to buy hay for the livestock. Turned out he had some bad investments, also had taken out a large loan at the credit union. His son was really ticked off when he found out. The guy was SO disappointed."

"But the boss man wanted to send you through college?"

"Yeah, and he did, in a way. I never graduated, but he left my mom and I some bonds. I worked hard, invested them. Took a year at college. Then my mom died. She'd never had the chance to have a good life. I crashed. Buried my mom, said goodbye to southern Alberta, and hit the road. Became a cowpoke for hire to anybody who'd take me." Ross looked distant for a moment. "Lots of prejudice, you know," he continued. "Even in Canada."

"How did you learn advanced math?" Cynthia edged a little closer to him on the sofa.

"Oh, I taught myself. Read Stephen Hawking, you know, different theories. The old boss was right. I was smart. You?" He moved toward Cynthia a bit, too.

"Oh, my father taught me. I thought, you know, I'm a girl, girls aren't good at maths, never tried, but he took me under his wing finally while I was doing O levels at school, and taught me most of what he knew."

Ross got up from the sofa and poured himself another gin and tonic. "How can you drink this stuff all the time? Who thought of mixing gin, lime and tonic water?"

Cynthia's face was flushed. Her nose was running a bit. "It treats malaria, taken with tonic water, which has quinine in it. The English invented that drink when we were in India." She grinned. "Not that we have malaria these days. But we Brits have learned to like our gin and tonic. We'll have another, Tex, won't we?"

Ross took the bottle from her hand. "I'm not superman," he said. "But when I saw you I said to myself, that woman is one special woman."

She ignored his drinking and pondered on what he'd just said. She glanced at his tall slim profile, with just a hint of a paunch above his belt buckle.

"What did your father do? Is he still alive?" Ross traced double lines of sweating moisture down the sides of his cold glass.

"My dad's an educated man. Oh, yes, still living. He's in a home in Devon," Cynthia said.

"Your mother?"

"Oh, she left years ago. I think she's dead." Cynthia became brusque. They both sat down again, closer to one another this time on the small pink settee with the satin cushions. Ross leaned back. He extended his arm along the edge of the back of the settee.

"My father taught theology at Cambridge. But he'd studied physics as well, in his undergraduate years. He liked to teach. So he taught me." Cynthia sipped on her drink.

"Both of us, self-taught," Ross said. "It's almost too much of a coincidence."

"Yes." Cynthia leaned her head against his arm. "My father's still brilliant, of course."

"Of course. No doubt about it," the cowboy said.

"He's in his eighties now."

"Still young," Ross said. He inched the fingers of his right hand along the curve of Cynthia's shoulder. His torn jeans and solid blue shirt looked very comfortable, and his hands were soft. Cynthia thought of loneliness and was it worth relieving it for a moment of pleasure? She noticed that Ross had shaved this morning. There was a hint of stubble beneath his chin, though. His features were rugged. Then he flung his arms back and stood up. Cynthia pitched to one side.

"What are you doing?"

Ross rubbed his black face. "Your father will kill me."

"Nobody will kill you," Cynthia said.

"My gosh, they'll all kill me."

"Oh, don't be so melodramatic," she said, slapping him on the seat of his jeans. "Cut it out."

"You don't understand." He sat down again and finished his gin and tonic in a couple of gulps. He wiped the moisture from his mouth and then got up and poured another drink.

"You don't understand," he repeated and took a stick of gum from his back pocket.

"It's racist," Cynthia said. "Is that it?"

"It's racist," he agreed.

"You're right." Cynthia saluted him. "They'll kill you. You're Scottish from the Hebrides. You told me when we met that your ancestors came from Scotland. Yes, and the Scots don't like the English, and you think we don't like you?"

That made him laugh. He stood with the glass in his hand and spilled some of it on the floor, chuckling so his hands shook and he couldn't finish his drink. Scottish from the Hebrides. Yes, he'd told her that. Ross was getting drunk.

"You're being pretty daft," Cynthia continued. "Do you think my brothers will lynch you?"

"Lynch me? You have brothers?" Ross became more sober.

"I have two younger brothers," she said. "Don't worry. They're both in India. And they don't care what I do as long as I'm happy."

"India?"

"Well, one's a missionary and the other one works in the British Embassy there. He's some kind of a consultant. Fun job."

"You ever been to India, Cynth?"

"Lots of times." Her pudgy white hands seemed artistic to him.

"My parents were in the Indian Civil Service in the 1950s," Cynthia said. "We traveled a lot." He understood then her attachment to her home, the one solid object in her life that gave her a sense of stability. He tried to explain his position.

"It's this way, ma'am. There's not a lot of intersecting lives between our two cultures. Two lives, parallel to one another, light years away at the start. Both start out at the same point but they're parallel and they don't connect. There's a life force there. A life source at the beginning that moves them along. And suddenly one of them gets a laser beam of excitement into his photons, into his being, and the other one veers away and then comes back and they think it's karma, but all it is, really, is that surge of power like a foot down on the gas pedal that's catapulted the two glowing lines of light into one another for a time. And if they're very lucky, they'll disentangle themselves and then move on, past the middle course, past the beginning, back, back to the future that's a circle where they might have started at one time and where it's okay to converge. Like looking at the back of your head. But if they veer off course too soon it's a disaster, see? It has to be predestined and at the right time in history. Not now. Not now, with the gin in us."

Cynthia patted the back of her head. Her hair was somewhat disheveled. "You're over- reacting, Ross. But you're right. I think this was all destined long ago, at the beginning where our lives like a ball of tangled string began to weave themselves into existence. We might think it's serendipity or coincidence, and maybe it is. But here we are, and if it was meant to be, maybe there's another Ross and another Cynthia in another universe who are meeting now as well, talking like this. And drunk..."

"Or maybe they've never met."

Ross hitched up his jeans and scowled. "For us, like the Prince of Wales at the tea, unlikely though it seemed, an appointment was set up at our births so it's possible for us to be together like this. Coincidence? No, I don't think so."

Cynthia sipped on her drink, but she was not very thirsty anymore. "I don't believe in destiny."

Ross grabbed the blowsy blonde woman and pulled her hair back, looking into her blue-green eyes. Then he kissed her, his lips gentle on hers. "I do. I *do* believe," he breathed. They kissed again, ebony and ivory.

There had been black-faced sheep farmed in Berkshire before the cowboy arrived, and a woolen cloth industry that dated from the Middle Ages. Other industries too: wine, nails, cottage industries, but mainly the woolen cloth. In the 21st century, Maidenhead was still a thriving town with buses, railroad, public services, industry, and resorts. It lies on the River Thames about twenty miles west of London.

Maidenhead in Berkshire will continue to exist as it has from ancient times. The conservationists will help and the Royals will live on in Windsor near the council houses in the Royal Borough of Windsor and Maidenhead. Nothing much will change although progress continues throughout the unfolding of the seasons and intersecting lives.

There's a school in Maidenhead and there little Mulatto children play with their friends. They eat hot lunches and talk of the singing bright bottles in the trees across from the pub, and how they got there.

They talk of the wild ponies back in Kent and the black, black man who was their father.

Knock, Knock the Robots Are Here

Ruby Dragon knew the Robot Apocalypse was real when a Hermes II model suffered a system failure as the machine was performing heart surgery on her husband, John. Ruby had been warned.

"Don't let any gummy-bear robot maestro work on John," her sister Sharon said. "Didn't the Hermes line spill hot coffee on Mom at the airport in Toronto?"

"A malfunctioning machine god," Ruby said. "It won't happen again."

"Huh."

"Seniors don't usually sue." Ruby pursed her lips.

"Mom did. The incident ruined her for life. Hot coffee in her lap and a million dollar lawsuit settled out of court. Steaming. Boiling. Coffee on her lap."

"True enough."

Hermes II, gleaming like a new razor, cut into John's chest. CyberCom CEO Justin Harper's image on the wall outside the Operating Room detailed robot safety regulations. Hadn't the OB/GYN robot Artemis delivered 1,534 new babies safely last year at the Civic Hospital? Hermes, precision forceps, parted John's sternum.

"Mom on her honeymoon at the airport in Toronto."

"Shut up, Sharon."

"Ruined for life."

"It won't happen to John. Hermes is safer than the cardiologist who..."

But the robot named after the God of the Caduceus malfunctioned in the OR at the Edmonton Civic Hospital; grasped John's fluttering heart in its meticulous digits and squeezed. That was not supposed to happen. The Hermes model had performed numerous valve replacement surgeries in the past year on patients like John; routine for Hermes II but too intricate for human intervention due to complications, as in the case of Ruby's obese (but handsome) and cigar-smoking husband John.

"We warned him," Sharon said. "Quit yer drinkin', quit yer smokin', quit yer high fat diet."

"It's not John's fault."

"No, Hermes failed."

The Robot's gleaming hands hadn't faltered until the end. Thus began the Robot Apocalypse.

Somewhere in a mine in Australia, a rock-busting robot grasped the head of its human foreman and cracked it like an egg. A StarBlue jet was diverted over Miami and flew into the Bermuda Triangle, never to be seen again; its robotic pilot and crew, and all human passengers, perished mysteriously in the roiling mists of the North Atlantic. The last transmission from StarBlue #10?

"Silicone Valley rules."

The CyberCom Company was very kind to Ruby and the rest of John's family. A lavish settlement was offered, an apology, a visit one afternoon to Ruby's condo in downtown Oliver. The CEO of the Artificial Intelligence Division of Toronto personally delivered the settlement cheque.

"We're working on humor," he said.

"Humor?" Ruby grimaced into the photographer's lens. Reporters hovered at the CEO's elbow.

"Yes, it's a new software program. It'll be a while before Hermes understands *advanced* humor. But he likes puns and knock knock jokes."

"You've got to be kidding."

"No. Here, sign this, Mrs. Dragon. It's a release."

"Release?"

The CEO tore the rubberized coating from his face and revealed a polished surface. "Surprise," it said. "I've been replaced by an Apollo Model IV."

"Sharon," Ruby said, and her sister came to the door.

"Well, do come in." Sharon had been listening. "I've often admired our government's take on humor. So glad the new overlords share it."

"Is your mother here?" The CEO removed its gloves and entered the condo. The robot's dexterity was impressive as it stamped the release, and massaged Ruby's back at the same time.

"Our mother passed away a month ago," Sharon said. "In Belize on her honeymoon. Rest in peace, mother. She was never to know a moment without pain after..."

"The coffee? Oh, yes, that unfortunate incident in Toronto perhaps predicted a problem with Hermes' competence. We're working on it now. Our robots should never have been serving coffee at the airport. Dangerous. That job should fall to humans, perhaps the Scots..."

"Oh, that feels good," Ruby said, arching her spine as the robot's fingers dug into the *latissimus dorsi* muscles of her back. "John used to do that. Rest his soul."

"Rest in peace, John." Sharon plugged in the electric kettle and put green tea leaves in the red Bodum. Ruby read the release, signed it, and the robot gave her a cheque for $1.5 million.

"The least we can do for the dreadful loss you've suffered."

"Oh, you fake sincerity, Apollo Model IV, but your hands are so deliciously *lithe*. I thought the same of Hermes II when I met him, but unfortunately, his hands failed as he operated on my husband."

"Yes, our colleague is in storage now, his circuits overloaded; he's been diverted to an EasyJet flight to Toronto for retooling. We think he'll be at the controls of a Boeing 737 next week. Much more intricate than surgery, of course, but we feel he's capable of so much more than that."

"What a good idea," Ruby said. Their old ginger cat wandered through the kitchen to its food bowl by the stove. Sharon poured boiling water into the Bodum. "Has Hermes Mk II been given a sense of humor?" she asked.

The CEO ran its hand over the speaker below its eye sockets and sat at the table. The photographer and reporters continued to snap pictures and ask intrusive questions.

"Our older models are being refurbished and provided with a primer of word play," the CEO replied. "A sense of humor if you like, based on relationships between words. The Apollo Model IV is capable of carrying on a conversation with humans replete with metaphors, subtle riposte and an intricate vocabulary database. And it drinks fluids."

The photographer tore off a lifelike plastic film to reveal a metal face. One of the reporters began to interview it. The photographer snapped some more pictures of the interior of Ruby's condo, focusing on a large print of John displayed on an east wall.

"Too bad," the photographer said. "Such a loss." The robot wiped an artificial tear from the corner of its eye socket.

Ruby folded the cheque and placed it in a drawer. Her sister and the CEO sipped their tea. A laptop stood on a desk in the corner and broadcast news from Corpus Christi. Hurricane Robert was approaching the Texas coast. Ruby knew the Robot Apocalypse had attained serious proportions when the image of a Hermes robot thrust TV reporter Dave Froehlich aside and began to broadcast from the streaming NBC station.

"The teacher told me to 'weed' during the summer so I went out into the garden." The CEO laughed and had another cup of green tea. "Read, get it?"

"My mother was seventy-four," Ruby said. "Too young to die."

Her sister Sharon pursed her lips and peered at the laptop. A hologram of Hurricane Robert swirled behind the broadcaster's metal head. The representation changed to show the interior of a Boeing

767. There seemed to be a disturbance in the cockpit as the faces of angry passengers confronted a Hermes model III.

"What's going on?" Ruby asked.

The photographer leaned into her face. "Excuse me. I work for the Evening Journal. You seem bewildered, Mrs. Dragon. May I help?" It snapped more pictures.

"Yes," a reporter said, digital recorder poised in its metal hand. "We're trying to keep records, Mrs. Dragon. Your husband was the unfortunate victim of a robot malfunction. There are sanctions in place against the company. Your representative is here to make amends. I've been programmed with an empathy chip. A statement?"

"Well," Ruby said. "My husband's gone. My mother's gone. I'm just overcome and bewildered." She paused. "Why don't you have a nose?"

The CEO sighed a programmed sound of compassion and went out into the world with its companions to continue negotiations.

"Knock, knock.
"Who's there?
"Dismay.
"Dismay who?
"Dismay not be a funny joke."

The robots laughed.

The men and women in Silicone Valley took off their plastic faces in 2018. That was the year Ruby's plane soared over Lake Superior on its maiden robot-staffed flight, with robot passengers, except for Ruby. She was on her way to Ottawa to meet the first CyberCom Prime Minister of Canada, Stephen Trudeau, a shadowy figure who appeared to spring up from myths and half-truths, and whom, she hoped, had a nose.

Her compatriots had improved so much in appearance during the past two years. It was almost like having John back again.

Short Circuit

The dentist's wife awoke with a head cold two hours before their house blew up. Her husband was a man of routine and left home at 7:45 a.m. He promised to call home at 10:00 a.m., no sooner and no later, his wife Quinn knew.

"Don't get up, darling," he said as he opened the French doors at the back, leading to the garage and pool.

"Id a minute. Shortly." Quinn reached for a tissue by the bed and laid her head back on the pillow. She heard the French doors click shut. Her eyes closed.

A few minutes later, she began to cough. She got up on one elbow and called for the Model 2000 Robot.

"Robot."

There was no response. Model 2000 couldn't speak but usually reacted promptly to a request. Except for this morning.

"ROBOT!"

The robot did all household tasks, and would even help her dress. Model 2000 had strong titanium arms with opposable thumb and fingers. It was powered by an internal electrical pack which delivered constant power to its metal frame, rubber wheels, and unique computing system or "brain", as Robotics Corporation called their latest refinement in artificial intelligence.

Whirrrrrrr. Model 2000 rolled to the edge of the bed then back from where it came.

"What IS the matter with you, 2000?" Quinn swung her legs over the edge of the bed. "Bring me a cup of coffee. And toast."

The robot returned with coffee, a glass of orange juice, and cookies. It rolled to the window and back, clutching at Quinn's arm. She shook off the robot's touch.

"Ged me my cigarettes."

The robot rolled across the room, crumpled Quinn's cigarettes into brown mush in its metal fingers and threw her lighter into the glass of juice. *Whirrrrrrr,* it propelled itself to the bedroom door. The dentist's wife shoved her feet into a pair of her husband's slippers and followed the crazed mechanical assistant with the complicated "brain" to the French doors.

"No, you don't," Quinn said. Her husband would hear of this when he called. The dentist would make short shrift of this mechanical monster. They had purchased the robot only six weeks before to help Quinn with the household chores. Quinn was fond of the device and imagined the robot felt likewise about her. Perhaps not, she thought this morning.

"Ged me my housecoat," Quinn said. Model 2000 returned with a pair of jeans and her husband's shirt. Quinn noticed the clock on the wall wasn't working. Had the power gone out? The robot raced to the oven and opened the door. What was it trying to tell her? Quinn couldn't smell the gas leak, nor did she suspect that a spark would result in an explosion.

"I'm going to take a shower."

She picked up her cell phone. *Whirrrrr clack clank whirrrrr,* the robot tore the phone from her grasp and doused it in her cup of coffee.

"Now that's enough!" Quinn reached for the desk phone. The robot grabbed it and laid the receiver down. *Whirrrrr clank clack.* It careened to the French doors and back to the large window in the kitchen, then to the dining room. Quinn followed it. The hands of the chime clock on the mantel began to turn towards the hour. The robot threw the clock on the floor where it broke into pieces. No human assistant would *dare* act this way, Quinn thought.

She didn't know the air was thick with Zylon gas, a new substance that was a hundred times more volatile than natural gas but much cheaper to produce, and artificially developed. Stores of it would last indefinitely. "It's safer than natural gas or nuclear energy," the salesman had explained. "Second only to solar or wind power." Quinn and her husband had the most modern appliances and equipment. Only the best, Quinn had thought, but they hadn't counted on a crazy robot out of control. *Whirrrrrrr.*

Their gas line was leaking and Quinn's nose was so stuffed she couldn't smell it. Model 2000 knew though. It calculated the time to 10:00 a.m. when Quinn's husband would call and precipitate a spark that would explode and destroy his home and wife. The robot knew there were other phones in the house. Its circuits whirred. There was a phone in the dentist's shirt which Quinn was wearing. Get rid of the shirt. It reached for the phone.

Quinn felt dizzy. Perhaps the robot was right by trying to get some fresh air? Quinn staggered toward the French doors and collapsed. The robot knew the phone would ring in ten seconds. No time. It scooped her up in its titanium arms and burst through the French doors to the pool. It was ten o'clock. The phone rang. A spark ignited the Zylon leak.

Ka BOOOOOMMMMM. Black clouds of smoke and a violent wind sucked the breath from Quinn as she and the robot dove into the deepest part of the pool, away from danger. Quinn shuddered and cried; she was safe in the middle of the pool. Model 2000 had saved her life. She was alone in the pool with that wonderful mechanical creature.

"I love you, 2000," Quinn said. The robot held her in its metal arms. She embraced the stalwart rigid frame, passionate in the transparent pool. The roiling warm water reached the robot's internal electrical system. It short circuited and 10,000 volts raced through Quinn's body.

Her husband and the fire department found them later that day, dead in the pool, the house a smoldering ruin. The garage remained intact.

"She had a short existence," her husband said at the funeral. He sued the Robotics Corporation for ten million dollars and rebuilt his house. The money scarcely seemed enough for his dear one's life. Model 2000 would have agreed, had it survived.

The Geese

Shards of sunlight glanced from the plane's huge silver wings onto the lake below. Penelope spotted the Canada geese from her window seat as the plane began to descend toward Houston International Airport. The shadow of the plane was blue on the lake and the geese were black dots. It was late November. Like the geese, Penelope, too, was wintering here. She was far from her home in Alberta, far from her reckless husband with his ice-blue eyes, far from the stillborn child in Edmonton, and the nurse who had wrapped him in his little white blanket and carried him away. Where was the scotched wee body now? Her husband had looked after the burial.

Penelope had wrapped herself in grief and buried her feelings with the coffin. The Manitoba maple leaves were yellow and orange, an early snow turning their Halloween decorations into ghosts.

"They're so majestic." Penelope's companion in the seat next leaned past her spare frame to look. "The geese."

"Not from here," Penelope said. She pushed her glasses farther up the ridge of her nose. They always slipped down like that, past the short aquiline crest, making her eyes appear larger.

"Did you know they mate for life?" Her companion shut the seat tray with a snap. An airline magazine lay on the expanse of her thighs. "I see them here every year at this time. Where do you suppose they summer?"

"I know that," Penelope said.

"Where?" her companion asked.

"I know they mate for life. But I know where they spend their summers, too. Same place as I do. Odd to see them here."

Penelope hadn't expected to see anything familiar 1,800 miles from home. The plane banked and prepared to land. She swallowed to relieve the pressure in her eardrums. Her companion leaned sweatily against her arm.

"This is the most dangerous time of the flight," the other woman said. "When we're landing or taking off."

"Canada," Penelope said. "They fly in autumn from my home in Alberta."

Penelope pulled the shade on the window to block the laser sun. Maybe if her husband hadn't braked behind the stopped car that afternoon in the middle of downtown Edmonton? If he'd pulled out and around it, kept going, so the vehicles at the traffic lights behind them had proceeded smoothly? If in the first place he hadn't insisted on buying that ridiculously tiny sports car with seats that split and crumpled when the truck hit them...

The baby that ripped from her body. The pain that fractured Penelope's whole being; the marriage that split just as surely, and Penelope now in an aircraft circling Houston International to find — what?

Relief from pain. She had made reservations for a hotel close to the airport, had vague plans of using her American visa to get a job here, escaping her marriage and the memories that went along with it.

It had been almost fourteen months. Penelope didn't think of it as an *accident*. Accidents weren't preventable; accidents were an Act of God; accidents didn't just happen in the middle of downtown traffic to a careful driver taking his pregnant wife home. Accidents happened randomly. This wasn't random. This was an outrage against her womb and all childbearing women who looked for protection from the reckless boys grown tall in the seat next to them.

Houston. They handled their luggage themselves, meager as it was, putting it on a cart and riding the long moving walkway from the terminal to the arrival zone.

A taxi driver wrestled the bags from Penelope's companion and stowed them in the trunk of his cab.

"Share the cab?" Penelope asked.

"Might as well," the dark woman said. "If you're not going anywhere special I know of an interesting hotel."

"The Texas Arms," the companion decided from the backseat of the cab. And she accompanied Penelope in the cab through the strange streets and byways on the way to their hotel.

It was noon and the traffic was heavy and rough. Trucks roared by, air brakes occasionally squealing. Penelope huddled in the seat next to her companion, who held a map of Houston.

"Turn here," the strange woman said to the man behind the wheel. "I chose it because it was close to the airport."

"I know it, ma'am." The driver was curt. Two fuzzy dice swung from his rearview mirror. A plastic Virgin Mary bobbed on the dash, blue and white like Penelope's coat. She endured the trip, feet thrust against the floorboards, shoulders tense.

"Slow down." Penelope gripped the seat. *No*, the baby in the cemetery, unnamed, her husband — foolhardy, thoughtless man. Cruel and thereafter distant.

"The light's turning yellow and it'll be red in a minute. It's not green anymore. You'll have to slow down." Penelope had a headache. Her curly brown hair barely extended above the back of the seat.

"What's the matter, lady? Ain't we got no colors y'all like?"

Her companion chuckled and folded the map.

"That's not funny," Penelope said.

"There it is," her companion said. "The hotel. I'm glad to see it."

"You was just thinking I was going to lead y'all a wild chase," said the driver. He wiped his face with a red bandana spotted with white dots, and turned off the meter. Penelope reached into her fake crocodile purse and paid him, leaving a big tip.

"Happy Thanksgiving, ma'am," the cabbie said.

"What?" Penelope asked.

"Thanksgiving's this Thursday," the companion said.

"Ours is in October." Penelope grabbed the luggage herself and trudged into the lobby. The companion followed mutely, lagging behind.

"What difference does it make?" Penelope asked. "October or November? Or not at all? Do I have anything to be thankful for?"

"Be thankful for your mistakes. You'll learn from them." The companion lifted an eyebrow.

"Mistakes." Penelope heaved their luggage past the glass doors of the Texas Arms. They booked a room with two doubles. "Nice of you," she said. "To see me here."

Much later they ate. Penelope had never tried southern food and gorged herself with chicken fried steak with cream gravy, biscuits, mashed potatoes, okra, and a large delicious sweet potato fritter. Her companion was quiet, half-hidden in the shadows.

Penelope's cell phone played *Dixie*. She had programmed the tune just before she'd left Edmonton. She held it to her ear.

He was breathing heavily. Her husband, drinking maybe; not usually a heavy drinker but tonight… she explained about her companion; how they had met on the plane and discovered they were two souls lost together screaming toward Houston at 500 mph and nobody to care or meet them. How they had reached out for one another, to share a hotel and perhaps the start of an adventure.

The silence stretched between Penelope and her husband like soft white snowflakes melting on her tongue from far away, another world.

"Come back," he said. "Come back, honey. You shouldn't have left. Did you hear the news about how the highway to Calgary was all snowed in, iced up, they said put on your chains, then a Chinook yesterday, a real warm wind from the east side of the mountains, temperatures went up forty-five degrees in an hour."

"So?" she said.

"Stay the weekend, come back on Monday, it's going to be a real nice winter here. Already starting out good here, and maybe we can go somewhere warm later on, what do you say?"

"Dave, I know you're not one to stay put even without me, in weather like that or not. If I know you, I don't think you're even home tonight. I'm in Houston and I'm going to stay here. It's their Thanksgiving Day tomorrow, Dave. I think I'll go swimming because we had Thanksgiving six weeks ago and I'm not grateful for anything. I don't want to celebrate with someone else's family or alone with our memories. It was easy to be grateful for the good things, once upon a time. But that's gone. Thanksgiving's a holiday for others this year."

There was silence on the other end of the phone.

Say something that will make me come back, Dave, she thought. But she knew he wouldn't or couldn't do that. He was trying his best but it wasn't good enough.

"Do you know why our Pilgrims ate turkey for Thanksgiving?" It was their favorite old holiday joke. Dave tried it one more time.

"Because they couldn't get the moose in the oven." Penelope smiled in spite of herself and pushed her glasses up the bridge of her nose.

"Nice of her to find you a room," Dave said. "Your new friend."

"She seems lonely." They promised to speak again and hung up.

Penelope draped a silver jacket over her shoulders and went exploring the outskirts of the hotel, by herself, and later her companion led her into the cool interior where they each had a double Margarita. Penelope eventually found herself drinking alone.

There was a sad old man playing one of twin pianos in the lounge until 11:30, then he left and Penelope was by herself.

The Texas Arms shut down around midnight. Her companion had long ago gone to their shadowy room. Penelope stumbled past the lobby up the stairs, opened the door onto the red worn carpet of the hallway on the second floor, the bulk of the soda machine next to the stairs; the row of identical doorways in front of her. She found their door and her key clicked in the lock. She leaned against the wall in the vast inner mysteriousness of their room until her eyes grew accustomed to the dim light. Her companion had gone to bed. A book by Marcus Aurelius lay open on the floor beside her sleeping form. Penelope picked it up. She was curious what other people read. Their thoughts were like the moon's landscape to Penelope, particularly those of this curious woman. Penelope knew only herself; her own thoughts, the claustrophobic workings of one mind. Sometimes not even that.

Marcus Aurelius didn't seem like anything Penelope would fly 1,800 miles to read.

Her eyes, dark as shadows, felt moist. She fell onto the soft down of the pillows on her bed. She lay there on her back, breathing precisely.

Their wedding — a gypsy bride, an Errol Flynn groom with borrowed finery, an officiate with crow's wings on his hat, the Renaissance linen scrolls with their home made marriage vows, and the wicked offbeat bouquets of flowers, berries, and weeds — seemed so long ago yet only four years. Dave had worn a feather in his cap.

Geese mate for life.

Her companion snored faintly in the next bed. The phone was silent. Why was she disappointed?

The next morning they rented a car and went to the Hard Rock Café in Bayou Place; they had no escorts for drinking and dancing at ROCBAR and were too shy to go alone. Penelope chose a t-shirt at the Hard Rock Café. They experienced zero gravity at the Johnson Space Center.

On subsequent days and weeks they took in the Houston Zoo and tried the waterslide at Splashtown; shopped in the Montrose district (nothing in common there), drove to the Downtown Aquarium and the Houston Museum District. They had brunch at the Cadillac Bar and enjoyed the beautiful waterfront view. Penelope was anxious about driving in cowboy-type southern traffic, but nobody shot at them because they cut somebody off or honked at them. She learned about staying on Westheimer and Montrose.

Her companion grew more quiet and often faded into shadows as night approached. Penelope's husband phoned often. She could tell he'd been drinking.

They moved to a vintage hotel in Old Town Spring. There was hot and hotter weather, alternated occasionally by a cool day. The humidity drenched their sheets when they opened the windows. How had people survived without air conditioning? They went to the beach on the Gulf. Hot and humid. Penelope began to long for home. Her companion sometimes seemed like an oil slick in Penelope's imagination, viscous, silent, dark. She seldom spoke anymore and only rarely accompanied Penelope to the piano bar or shopping, or to the entertainment parks where Penelope whooped down the waterslides and rode the bumper cars until twilight.

Her husband continued to call. Penelope could tell he'd been smoking again as well as drinking. His voice was ragged.

One day there was a child in the hotel. Just a baby, hardly able to stand, a little girl dressed in striped pink rompers with a yellow bow in her curly sparse blonde hair. Chubby red cheeks and eyes blue like Dave's but not ice-blue; rather robin's egg blue if anything, and soft skin like the touch of feathers.

The baby's mother liked to party and would leave the baby alone in her old growling car while she drank with her friends at the Jailhouse Saloon. The companion definitely didn't like this and in a rare outburst, told Penelope so and that she must do something about it or risk something bad happening to the child. It would be on Penelope's head forever, she said. So Penelope arranged with the mother to care for the baby. She named her Rosebud. The baby's mother called her simply, "the baby". Penelope didn't know the baby's birth name. If she had one.

One morning the mother didn't come back. The desk clerk checked her room two days later. She had gone, with her old battered luggage and a bottle of whiskey. Penelope and the companion didn't call the authorities. They waited for the mother to come back. They waited for a long time.

Rosebud began to call Penelope "mommy". Penelope's husband stopped sending them money in February.

Penelope got a job bookkeeping for the hotel. Her friend looked after the child while Penelope worked. Penelope wore tee-shirts on the weekends and took Rosebud for walks. The companion grew more silent and one day Penelope went looking for her and didn't find her. She had slipped into the mysterious viscera of the city.

Penelope's husband didn't call anymore. She registered Rosebud for daycare.

In March the geese left.

The Ham Sandwich

The Peace River country in northeastern British Columbia is known for hearty meals, but in my mother's opinion, nothing ever surpassed The Ham Sandwich.

Striding bravely through the snow at 48° below, my mother and I got off the train in Pouce Coupé in the middle of January 1946. I was eighteen months old and in her arms. I had been fed but she was ravenous. The Second World War had ended a few months before and my soldier father was delayed as his discharge papers had been lost. We were city girls, my mom and I, from Toronto. My mother was a Registered Nurse who had given up her career and home in Ontario to marry a handsome soldier/farmer from the Peace River country (frozen ten months of the year like the Frozen Logger). She had traveled with me thousands of miles on a coal-fired train to be reunited with her husband; money was in short supply on the trip, and she had barely eaten the expensive meals on the train.

Her new sister-in-law met her at the station. They were to become lifelong friends, long after both husbands had died in their seventies. But then all my mother knew was she was very hungry after the long cold train trip, and I needed milk.

Now in the East, a ham sandwich is a pitiful thing, two thin slices of white bread enveloping a slippery allotment of something pink and transparent, accompanied by a soggy piece of lettuce and perhaps, to the fortunate mendicant, some equally slippery cheese.

But this was the North where men were men, and women were, too; and they'd eat a bale of hay if you poured sugar on it. But there had to be a lot of it, and it had to be good.

Thus The Ham Sandwich my mother ordered at the train station blew off her white stockings. Everything about The Ham Sandwich was big and satisfying. The bread was homemade and fresh, and sliced by hand to a couple of inches thick. Texas Toast? This was genuine Northern British Columbia Leavened Bread, with real butter a quarter of an inch thick slathered over the surfaces of two slabs of bread; hard Canadian cheddar cheese sliced extravagantly and piled on the culinary masterpiece: The Baked Ham! Oh, the Ham! My mother talked about this sandwich to the end of her life. She lived to be 91. The Ham was thick and juicy; pink but not too pink, marbled with fat which was *so* good compared to these anorexic protein offerings of today; fat but not too fat, slow roasted to perfection, carved with care and lovingly heaped on the thick white bread and swirls of creamy butter, dribbled with Keen's yellow mustard and *heated*.

I never did hear whether I got my milk.

The Minotaur

The small college campus was modern, concrete, landscaped, green, and there was a new building, long and narrow, grey and sprawling. Here in the longest and most jutting wing was the Division of Classical Scope where Ariadne worked. A plaster cast of Greek gods hung on the wall and on a table lay a small statue.

These were scholarly and civilized people, though their philosophy and languages were lifted from the bones of a long-dead race of murderers, mythmakers and prophets, their spirit, for the most part, dead as dust.

But not all, at least, that should have been, was gone.

One day something very different came to life within the halls, moved about the halls in blindness like a mole, at first. Invisible, its chromosomes were a code in ancient script, born perhaps from some spirit of old books or ancient lore, dropped from dreams of hot Cretan sun and labyrinth, of palaces and youths whose blood was hot and sweet and kindled that strange rage that moved within the creature like a thirst. The head and shoulders of a bull snorted on the torso of a fine Olympian athlete. Its arms as they swung almost touched the walls on either side of the corridor; the great legs were knotted and braced against the weight which they had to support; the head was a furnace of might as it moved from side to side, taking in its surroundings with dull wondering eyes that signified the presence of an intelligence less than a man but more than a beast.

It was the Minotaur. He looked about him, confused. People moved and spoke quietly in the room into which he stepped, but his presence was no more than a shadow or a chill in the face of noon. They couldn't see him.

His emotions glinted like jewels. Their disbelief pricked his fear and anger bright as coals, sent him hot and reeling to the walls that smoked against his touch. He buckled like a boy, back he fell before the terrible omniscience and calmness of their ignorance. He fell against the farthest wall; his eyes were red with hate. No one paid him any mind.

"Theseus!" he roared and many little flakes of plaster settled gently on his brow, like snow. He sat huddled against the wall and watched the sunlight glitter against the glassed shelves opposite. The blurred and static books did not blame or pity, censor or scorn him; neither did they believe. They merely cried in little terms of that thing priceless, huge and glittering, dancing in their midst; that of brain. This did not spawn him, beast of little priceless brain, but guts and dread of heart. So he sat.

When day fell like a sigh towards evening, the Minotaur rose and moved through locked doors, as if a wraith, to the top of the outside steps that led from the main doors of the Division of Classics to the street. No one was aware of him as a presence in the shadows of the night and he slept a little, sprawled against the doors of the building. Three thousand years old his dreams became, and gave him little comfort.

As he rumbled in his sleep, Theseus chased him like a dog through alleyways of sky. Fearful constellations broke upon new eons as the Minotaur ran. Troubled in his sleep, the Minotaur pitched about, his monstrous body a darker blot beneath the stars than the blackness of the night. In his dreams he pounded, through the eons, as the constellations wheeled beneath his feet. His hands dripped blood and his mouth was a furnace of dread. The stars tipped and burned, and roared beneath his feet. He lost his balance, slipped and fell.

He lay crumpled at the foot of a mighty cross. The taste of the flesh that in his life had sustained him, the flesh of Greek youths, was in his mouth, the taste of wetness; hot exciting, sacrifices ripped from grieving mothers' arms, the hotness of the Minotaur was on his breath, the blanket of evil on his shoulders wrapped itself about his eyes and mouth, and crushed him almost to a second death. The Cross was illuminated as though from within; it was huge and extended upward far above his head as he lay prone at its base.

"Theseus!" he roared.

Goodness and mercy... surely goodness and mercy... where did it say that – the noise was deafening. He covered his ears. The holy Cross above him burned with a cold intensity. And then, ever so slowly, it began to creak. It began to sway. And it fell. *All the days of my life...*

"Theseus!" he cried, "Save me!" A light burst before him and he could barely see.

The light was a thousand suns upon the Minotaur's face. The heavy Cross with the awful light fell toward him, and upon him, with a strange whistling sound as it fell, and he shattered the calm of the morning where he slept as he covered it with his screams.

That morning there was a great storm and the clouds were driven like madness in the face of the sun as it rose. But the Minotaur did not awake. His body flowed like vapor into the air, and his voice was lost in the howl of the wind.

Grandmother's Story

Mark was cute, and Cindy in the 1950s was a loser with a pimple on her chin and her shoes were too big. Her mother bought large shoes so she would "grow into them". Cindy was in grade 10. She annotated her books perfectly. Her teacher was very proud of Cindy's skill with the highlighters. Annotating books was the only thing Cindy did well, and she was proud of it too, the yellow stickers, the pink and blue highlighters, the weird looks from her classmates who would rather flirt at South Peace High, behind their hands. Behind the teacher's back. Cindy was the 'teacher's pet', her classmates giggled. Cindy had one good friend in high school, and they both liked Mark.

Her friend's name was Julie. Julie did not use deodorant. Cindy didn't like that but she didn't say anything because Julie was her best friend. They used to hide under their desks at school when the Air Raid sirens blared over the town. There was something called the Cold War between Russia and the USA in 1957. Cindy was afraid of the A-Bomb.

Mark's father had died when Mark was ten, and the boy worked in the family store up on the hill leading to the mall. Mark wore acrylic sweaters too big for him. He was an honors student in Cindy's class. She didn't see much of him because he worked almost all the time when he wasn't going to class. They took the same bus to the mall after school.

One day Cindy screwed her courage to the point where courage squeaked, and she told Julie she smelled. Then she took the bus to the top of the hill. She opened the door of the small store where Mark worked. His back was to her. He was stocking shelves with canned goods, Italian tomatoes and canned beans. His mother was at the counter.

"May I help you, dear?" His mother smiled at Cindy. Cindy took her glasses off, squinting.

"Y-yes," Cindy stammered. Luna moths, brilliant but invisible, erupted in her stomach. Mark turned around. His dark eyes laughed at hers on this fourth October 1957.

"I'd like a small gift for someone." Cindy swung her borrowed Bay bag from her shoulder. "My mother asked me to get a frilly baby card."

"A baby card?" Mark's mother smiled again.

"Y-yes."

"Perhaps a little gift?"

Mark was watching her.

"Maybe." Cindy's stomach flopped.

"Mark, can you help this young girl, please?" His mother turned to an elderly customer who had just walked in the door. "Perhaps you two know each other from school."

"I've seen her around." Mark heaved a box of canned soups to the top shelf.

"My name's Cindy."

"You're in my class. Can I help you, Cindy? Here, this might be what your mother needs." Mark reached out and touched her hand. Invisible sparks flew from the tips of his fingers to hers. She looked down. He was holding a pink baby card and a little sweater.

"It's perfect," she said.

Mark grinned. "It's not for you?"

Cindy blushed. "Of course not."

Just then Julie walked in the door. Julie smelled good. Cindy took a step back.

Mark was cute and Cindy was a loser with a pimple on her chin, and her shoes were too big. Even Julie looked better than she did. Cindy

40

bolted through the door of the small store, sobbing. Julie followed her. Mark stood in the doorway.

"Meet you after work?" She heard him call.

"Who?"

"Well, you, Cindy, of course. If it's okay with your mom. I get off work at eight. Meet you at the mall food court?"

The Luna moths in her stomach collided with the butterflies, and she almost danced.

"Yes!" she shouted. "Yes, yes."

Mark sure was cute. Julie sure was jealous. Cindy's feet were light all the way down the hill. Annotating books was the only thing Cindy did well. But she could learn.

Sputnik circled the Earth and Cindy danced on fourth October 1957.

In 1964 she and her best friend Julie saw Dr. Strangelove together. They had learned to stop worrying and love the bomb.

How They Met

Sunday, Valentine's Day 1965. She thinks of her death, above the silver river, ice sparkling like an early communion cup. There are only rails to stop her below the rumble of a train, while at the other end the road turns and then the open hill.

Uncertain, she will jump—but a figure on a bicycle is watching her. Daylight flecks a pockmarked face, half shaded, alien to her as moonscapes. He has come on his black and silver Schwinn to seek the fishes at the bottom of the glaciered river. Metal-clanging morning, snow still packed, like their dreams, fragile as a prayer. A resolute despair has brought them here, the man and woman. Together in a final, quite unlikely coupling.

Uncomfortable with self-consciousness, she tilts her chin to the struts above. The grey ringing cage of bridge encompasses both of them. Train sounds and flakes blow from the world of those still unaware. Still she does not move. He gazes at her with his amber eyes. Quiet as a cat, he pads closer, from the tent of shadow, to her. There's nothing more to do than hold his hand and run, by the frost-drenched rails, into a tomorrow of endless Sundays.

Your grandmother and your grandfather met on the High Level Bridge, child. That was when they stood like icons on the side of acrid memories — and did not jump.

Indeterminate Time in Hell

"Isn't this great?" the new little spirit said, in her short skirt and green plaid jacket.

"Yeah," her friend with the pajama bottoms and spiked boots replied.

"Whaddya mean?" The young man with blue spikey hair and a ring in his lip looked through his transparent hand.

"I mean our souls were just drawn up like a moth to a candle flame. Only two minutes ago we signed a suicide pact and overdosed."

"Whaddya mean?" The young man with the ring in his lip flexed his black wings.

"I mean isn't this awesome?" The new lithe spirit blew on her freshly-applied nail polish. "Here we are, in a *good* place. Wonder if there's anything to inject."

"This place makes me nervous." Her friend in the pajama bottoms glanced over her shoulder. "Like, there's *nobody* else here."

"Just us." The young man's eyelids drooped.

"Clouds everywhere," Mini Skirt said. "Must be heaven."

"Say, let's ask *her*." Pajama Bottoms spotted a tiny figure in the distance, looming larger as it approached them.

"Who?" Ring in Lip looked around.

"*Me!*" The Fury gibbered, and *thrust the Gorgon's head among them.* They immediately turned to stone. But they could still feel, and experience sensations and emotions.

Sensations like that of burning flesh. Singed hair. Scorched, bubbling and blackened skin. Always, as they tumbled in opposite directions from one another and were forever separated. For an eternity, without friends or companions, an agony of loneliness. Burning forever, as they fell through a hole in the sky that sucked them to a pit of snakes below in a pot of living quicksand. Their immobile and immortal bodies gasped for breath.

They were young. But they suffered the unbearable agony of remorse, endless and burning regret, terror, separation and loneliness. It should have been forever.

But their gentle Maker longed to end their torment. On a day of mild love they were snuffed out by his merciful hand. No more remained of Mini Skirt. Pajama Bottoms. And Ring in Lip.

They had mothers who cried. Fathers who cried.

Their friends on Earth hung flowers on their houses and later screamed from a burning pit. Their turn had come.

Perversion

They met at night, in a darkened bistro down a darkened alley. Cisco wore a black shirt and tight black pants with chains, trying to fit into the main culture of post-apocalypse Northwest America. She would be waiting for him there, dressed as a man.

The server knew them. He met Cisco at the door; put a finger to his lips.

"Shhh, my friend. The cops were here earlier."

"Did they arrest anyone?"

"No one. We were discrete."

"Is she here?"

"Yes. There, at your usual table by the back door."

Even with her hair pulled back severely under a felt fedora and her slight frame encased in a man's coat, Andrea was beautiful. Cisco caught his breath. Their love was forbidden by the State. They met here as they could and sometimes later slipped upstairs to one of the rented rooms.

"I'm frightened by the intrigue," she whispered, holding out a white hand to cover his brown one. "We will be found out one day."

"I know." He swallowed the absinthe that swirled in a dirty glass in his other hand. "We have to make a decision, Andrea. Run away to Canada."

"The underground railway is long and dangerous. I've heard we're often turned back at the border."

Perversion

"It's a risk we have to take. I can no longer live this way, with glimpses of you at night, living a lie during the day."

"Me, too, my darling. I've heard in history…"

"Yes. In history things were turned around. We weren't hunted for our aberration. We were rewarded and our love was the norm."

"I can hardly believe it."

"It's true. In the late 20th century and early 21st century, before the apocalypse brought about by the fundamentalists who believed a lie…"

"Or are we the lie, my darling?"

He ordered another absinthe. "Here in Westboro we are relatively safe, Andrea, but is that safety a façade, and if so, how long will it last? If we flee to Canada we will be amongst the norm."

A snake of moisture glistened down her cheek. The waiter approached to take their glasses.

"We're closing down early tonight," the waiter said. "Cops have been spotted not two blocks away, coming this way again."

"I won't be a criminal," Andrea cried. She took Cisco's hand. "Marry me, darling. It's legal in Canada."

"I've heard once our love was the norm," Cisco said. "May we find happiness, Andrea."

He was a man and she was a woman, in a society of homosexuals.

"Let's fight hard," he said. "We must make heterosexuality legal."

Then the cops broke down the door.

The Devil and His Imps, Indeterminate Time

"Bosh," the Devil said to his favorite imp, and leaned on his throne, a thousand leagues below Edmonton, Canada on a warm afternoon.

"Yes, boss?"

"I want you to explain to me what the Greek, Tantalus, is doing down here?"

"Why, he's rolling a great stone up the slopes of yon mountain," the imp said.

"And then?"

"Why, the stone rolls down again when it's two feet from the top."

"And his task?"

"To get the great stone to the top of yon mountain." The imp grinned, proud that he knew the answers.

"Great fiddlesticks!" The Devil slapped both hands on the arms of his throne. "That's it, then!"

"Yes, boss?" Bosh grinned again, wanting to please.

"That's the answer," the Devil said. "I must tell God."

"T-T-Tantalizing, isn't it?" Bosh screwed up his little black face. He gesticulated to the other imps, who ran away from behind the throne.

"Tantalizing indeed. Rolling that great stone."

"I knew that."

"We all knew that," the Devil said. "But did we think about it?"

"Think about it." Bosh placed a finger on his chin.
"Think."
"I know."
"What?"
"It rolls down again." Bosh beamed.
"And then?" The imps hugged themselves.
"He has to start all over!"
"And *then*?" The Devil pressed the gold elevator button for 'Way Up'.
"He gets two feet from the top."
"Then? What next? And then?"
The imps hugged themselves again. "The great stone rolls back down the mountain," they sang together.
"He has to start all over!" The elevator doors closed behind their fiery boss.
"THINK," Bosh said.
The imps scattered and began to throw coals at an image of a TV celebrity. "You're so vain," they chanted. Not the real thing. Yet.
"It's the answer to life." Beelzebub was on his way to meet the Big Boss. The elevator's indicator read 'Heaven' and an alarm went off. Time telescoped.
"The answer is..." He was in Heaven only long enough to find the answer.
The indicator light read 'Ground' then winked out. The elevator doors opened and Beelzebub spilled out. Time was relative in Hell and Paradise.
"What's the question?" the bravest of the demons asked. He pushed Bosh's face into the fire. Another imp sat at a computer console and typed in a code. Flames whipped across the screen. The celebrity's face appeared. The imp smiled.
"Let me out," the celebrity said. The imp pushed Delete and his face vanished.
"There. That's it."
"The answer to life." A large demon drank lava from a cup.

"God said we could continue." Lucifer strode to his place on the throne. "I wonder what He meant by that?"

"We get two feet from the top…"

"And we *start all over.*"

"The answer is in the question. It's all a matter of relativity."

"Say, do you think we could ask Job?"

"No, he's not here."

"So who's here we could ask?"

"They're all converting to the Big Boss upstairs. None of the top scientists here. Well, a few maybe. The older generation. Galileo and the three spies, guys like them. They're here. But lately? Nobody. Not even Stephen Hawking. No one who would know the meaning of life."

"Who would know, then?"

All eyes turned toward Satan. He drummed his fingers on his throne, an old electric chair which was quite useless as there was no electricity in Hell.

"You need a better throne, boss."

"I had four of these things. We gave three to Texas, who could use them."

"You should've gave that one to Alabama, boss. This is hell. We don't need no electric chair. We got to wait for the South to fry them."

"It's like the story of the fish," the Devil said to his imps and demons. He tapped his fingers.

"Two men, Wa-wa and Chi-chi, were once walking together along a road. They came to a bridge. They were halfway when they stopped and looked over the side at a school of fish swimming in the river below.

"Wa-wa said to Chi-chi, 'Why do you think the fish are swimming below, Chi Chi?'

"Chi-Chi answered, 'I, standing here, think it is the pleasure of the fish.'

"They were silent for a moment.

The Devil and His Imps, Indeterminate Time

"Then Wa-wa said, 'Why do you, standing there, think it is the pleasure of the fish?'

"Again they were silent.

"Chi-chi answered, 'Why do you, standing there, ask me why I, standing here, think it is the pleasure of the fish?'

"More silence.

"Then Wa-wa said, 'Why do you, standing there, ask me why I, standing here, ask you why you, standing there, think it is the pleasure of the fish?'

"They went on this way back and forth for a while until suddenly they stopped and Chi-chi said, 'What was the original question?'

"Wa-wa said, 'I asked, why do you, standing there, think it is the pleasure of the fish?'

"They both fell silent again. Then Chi-chi said, 'I believe, if you will consider it well, the answer to your question is in the question.'

"They fell silent again.

"Then Wa-wa and Chi-chi smiled at one another and walked arm-in-arm off the bridge and down the road again."

The Devil stopped his story and smiled, a dreadful thing to see. Bosh was playing a mindless and violent game on his tablet. He munched on a hot coal.

"Deep."

"Exactly." Satan glanced about for reassurance. "That's what the Big Boss told me."

Whhsssshhhh, Thud, Crash, Wheeeee, Thud. The computer game absorbed them all. "What else did he say, boss?"

"Do it myself."

The celebrity smiled through the flames. Alabama and Texas cheered.

The Preacher in Osoyoos

The Reverend Sheridan Day contemplated the tree. The pearl tree thrust up from the desert in Osoyoos, beautiful, unexpected. Each pearl on the brown dead branches held a soul. How lovely and how perfect.

Sheridan Day had been raised in the Methodist Church, then United, now he was Independent, an evangelist crying in the wilderness of television. He knew he was a hypocrite. He knew the Mayan prophesy was a fake but he used it to his own advantage. The physicist and the three computer experts believed in Sheridan Day and his sincerity. Used to adulation, he had journeyed into the desert of Osoyoos to escape the stress heaped on him by the approach of the end of the world as he knew it. He knew it wasn't the end of humanity nor the end of the solar system; it wasn't the end of the universe; it was simply the end of a world age. In that way the prophesy was correct.

The Reverend Day had made his pact with the Devil at the beginning of his ministry, promising to deliver souls in exchange for power, gold cars, and beautiful women.

His wife was the most beautiful woman he had ever seen outside the wide screen of movies. She was devoted to him and a good mother. She was the perfect hostess. Sheridan hated her. She kept him from his dream of ultimate freedom, tied to her with bonds of perfection and fidelity. She gave him no reason to desert her. His particular dream of authority now was tied to the conspiracy beneath the mountain of

Mufindi in Africa, the writhing atoms of a living computer that would destroy Sheridan's earth. That his wife and family would perish, too, was of little concern to the Reverend. He would live, and the power he had sought would be his.

"Whisht, fella." The tree whispered in a dry warm breeze that sounded like words. Irish words, and the Reverend remembered his grandmother from Eire, the humor, the songs, the warmth, the mellow biting whiskey that destroyed his maternal grandmother's family all *twisted* and *sozzled*, as she liked to say in her broad brogue. Sheridan had not drunk alcoholic beverages for twenty-three years, since his early twenties, after the twelve-step programs and the violent conversion in an evangelical circus tent that day in 1989 when he'd found the dead bird by the side of the road, buried it, and went on to repent of his sins before a crowd of hundreds.

Maria was his wife's name. She bore him three perfect children; a daughter and two sons, one in middle school, one in high school, the eldest (a boy) in trade school learning electronics. Sheridan thought his son could do better and told him that often, but his son, bright faced, smiling, gave him no further trouble than that. Maria told him there was no nobler profession than working with one's hands. Perhaps she was right. The Reverend had no formal post-secondary education himself and had wished more for his children and got it; a good trade school, the very best high schools and high marks.

Sheridan and his family had the life of a leprechaun who's found the end of the rainbow.

So why was he in the desert outside of Osoyoos now, contemplating the pearl tree?

"Whisht, man." Yellow eyes of the Devil gazed into his. "Each pearl is a soul trapped in perfection, layered in hard shells of beauty, centers hard as bone with putrid marrow."

"I see," Sheridan said and caressed the rock from which the tree sprang.

"Each is a soul you've trapped."

"I see. I'm brought here in my gold Mercedes to see the results of my preaching over the years? From the beginning, haven't I produced a living organism?"

"Only Maria and your children are products of your humanity."

"That seems harsh."

"Now that your ministry is at its apex, it's right that you should crack the secret of your success in the path you chose."

"I know the secret. I sold my soul to You for success."

"Yes, Sheridan. But do you know the secret of it?"

"It lies in the other side of the world, in more wretched souls than these trapped in a living computer that'll destroy the world as I know it. It is a wretched and evil place. It doesn't deserve to live."

"No, Sheridan. *You* don't deserve to live."

"This tree?" He asked of the Devil.

The sun warmed the pearls like seedpods and they cracked open. A worm fell out of each center.

"Those are the souls you've saved, Sheridan."

"But they looked so beautiful."

"You think your wife is beautiful?" The creature with the yellow eyes extended a huge claw to Sheridan. In the center of its palm was a cabbage moth. The moth fluttered its wings and attached itself to Sheridan's shirt. He brushed it away. As it flew, a large falcon swooped from the eye of the sun and devoured it.

"Life is like that," the Devil said. Sheridan bowed and fell on his face.

"I worship you, great creature," he said. "You've shown me the meaning of my life."

The pearl tree rustled, its branches stripped.

"Go back and do what you must," the Devil said. "Destroy what others have made."

"I will."

"You always have endeavored to create. This time you must tear down."

"No. I see now. I made only sand castles."

"Who are you, Sheridan?"

"I serve you, great Beelzebub."

"You are a servant, then?"

"Yes. I'm a servant of that which I purport to destroy. In the middle of midnight I worship you."

"Why?"

Sheridan was silent.

"My brothers are curious."

"I think I'm on the winning side."

"That's all?"

"No. I value power and pride. My training prepares me for that, yet humility is the standard."

"So you've found—"

"Yes. I've found the way to achieve my goals in this life and forever."

"Forever, Sheridan?"

The golden orbs shone on the evangelist prostrate in the desert. A hot wind moved the empty pearl tree. From each pearl a worm grew and nibbled on Sheridan Day. Sand choked his mouth and he was unable to scream.

His gold Mercedes filled up with silica gel.

In their home a few dozen miles away, Maria waited for her husband to come home. He did not come home that day nor the next, and eventually they found him in the desert, choked with sand and cold as a locker in the morgue.

The End

*In memory of my son Steve
who liked hard science fiction and William Gibson's novels*

The transformer heater fit into the freeze plug and that meant draining the engine of its nuclear fuel, popping off the reactor cover, hoisting the device on a mount and inserting the heater. Curtis, the captain on the botched mission to the Andromeda star system, was no mechanic, and he was in charge of the metallic object that had brought the Earth station to this icy planet.

Major Robert Gibson parachuted down to the tip of the glacier where the device rested. The tags on his dilanium suit folded over his ample frame and the gloves snapped well up on the elbow hinges. His titanium boots weighed almost nothing in the surprisingly low gravity of BlueStar II. The super had told him it wasn't necessary to wear his helmet but Robert was careful. He had seen what happened to careless men on missions such as this.

"Horny little Andromedans been swarming over us like Venusian roaches on a marsh stew," the captain said. "Glad you're here, Major. I need a replacement worse than Carl Sagan needed a telescope and camera."

"What happened? Terminal engine froze solid on its re-entry, did it?"

"Ya. We were lucky. No casualties, just a touch of frostbite when Vega dropped over the horizon for the short night. This hunk of frozen rock is about the size of Jupiter but synchronized with its star to pull gravity so it's like bouncing through marshmallows. You don't need that helmet, ya know. O^2 dust from around Vega penetrates the atmosphere here on BlueStar II so it's like breathing rarefied air."

Robert motioned toward the toolbox and computer chips embedded in his suit. "I'll run a scan."

"You don't need to run a scan. It's obvious what's wrong. The thing is frozen solid and even the plutonium inside isn't enough to keep the mechanical parts moving."

"Yeah, the flanges are seized."

"Where's the ship you came planet-side on?"

"It's hovering straight above." Robert pointed to a blue dot in the atmosphere. "Just a robocraft from the Mothership."

"An escape pod? How do I get back? I been here longer than Albert Einstein let his hair grow."

"They'll pick you up. I'm in charge now, Captain. Where are the others?"

Curtis gestured. "Under the mountain. We found caves heated with thermal currents from deep underground. We had enough food supplies and equipment. The women are arming themselves against the Andromedans. It isn't safe out here for them, sir."

"I think I understand. Where do they come from and what happens when I get the engine going again?"

"We'll use it for power, of course."

"I know that. But we're sharing this planet with a bunch of...?"

"Horny Andromedans. They're all wraiths, like ghosts, but solid enough, if you get my drift. We don't know where they come from. There was nothing here when we crash-landed two months ago and now they're everywhere. Ugly violet creatures with seven sexes."

"Seven sexes?"

"We're the eighth and ninth."

"Oh, I think I see. What do you do to fight them off? Do they know we're... er..."

"Not interested? Oh, yes."

"Interesting." Robert bent over the engine and took a long slim object out of the toolkit on his chest, popped the cover off the reactor port and peered inside.

"Going to be a cup of soup," he said. A winch unrolled from the pack on the chute and hoisted the engine off the ice. He wriggled under the engine and fitted a cap over the plutonium basket, removed the fuel containers and pulled out the freezer plug.

"Look at this, completely trashed," Robert said. He reversed the procedure, inserted the heater cartridge, threw away the freezer plug, transferred the plutonium back to its case, screwed on the port cover and tamped it down with the shaft of a special tool.

"The head of ice is going to melt soon," Robert said. The winch purred and the engine settled again into place on the tip of the glacier.

Curtis shook his head. "Get me out of here."

A woman, laser gun smoking and spitting light, appeared in an opening in the mountain behind them. "There they are. Son of a brown sugar patty. There's more of them every day, I swear."

Ka-boom! She was thin and danced over the ice fields. Robert squinted. He could see no one else.

"Where are they?" he asked.

"Why, Bob, they're all around us." Curtis began to swat at the viscous air. "There, you see. They're everywhere."

Robert scratched his head through the open faceplate in the helmet.

"If you say it's time you went Earth-side, I'd agree, Captain," he said. "I'll call the pod."

"Don't you see?" Curtis clutched his arm. "I can't leave the women like this."

"I'll take care of it."

"You're my replacement?"

"Yes. We've been worried. The transmissions from BlueStar II since you landed have become increasingly erratic, Captain. I was told to advise you of that. You're relieved of your command right now."

"Relieved?"

"Yes, Captain. Nothing to worry about. I'm here to take over."

"All by yourself?"

"How many men are here altogether?"

"We have five men and three females at the station. It's the females I'm worried about, sir."

Ka-boom. The thin woman danced back over the ice, gun flaming and face afire with purpose.

"What's she doing?"

"Why, she's destroying the Andromedans. Don't you see? They're after her."

Robert pulled on his lip through the open faceplate. He punched a few buttons in the palm of his glove and the robocraft responded, hovered several hundred feet above the three humans.

"Get in," he said.

"Where?"

"The port is open. We'll winch you up."

"Winch?"

"Yes. It's a multipurpose machine. Let me strap you in."

"Goodbye, Major Gibson."

"Goodbye, Captain. Better luck on your next mission."

"Oh, crap."

"What?"

"Now they're all over me." Curtis swatted the fetid air.

The woman hoisted her laser gun to her shoulder and fired several rounds. Blue sparks snapped across the winch as it swung the Captain up to the descending pod. Robert watched as the dilanium-suited officer was transported through the opening in the small craft and the port slid shut.

"Good," he said, and spoke again into the number pad on his glove. "Now hear this, Mothership. Seal off the area and don't let anyone down. I'm going to investigate. Possible alien involvement. Repeat. Possible alien involvement."

The woman stared into the dark sky as Andromeda appeared to rapidly circle its massive planet.

"Too late," she said.

"Too late?"

"They're with him."

"With the Captain?"

"They're all around him, yes, sir. Can't you see it?"

"What?"

She ground the freezer plug under her boot and aimed the gun at the booster engine. The ice was melting. The engine was probably serviceable and would support the station for a hundred years without replacement.

"What are you doing? Don't, that's an order, soldier, miss."

"We can't let them get away."

More shapes were striding toward them from the cave in the side of the mountain. Human beings, bent and shuffling from the weight of huge laser guns.

"Is that all you brought with you to the surface?" Robert was curious.

"There they are. Holy cornflakes," one man said. He aimed his gun at Robert's groin.

"You're all crazy," Robert said. "I'm your Captain's replacement. Stand to attention and that's an order, soldiers. Head Office on Earth wants to know what's happening here. I have a report to complete. You're going to help me."

Later, the violet wraiths surrounded Robert and nibbled at his chest. When they got to his throat it was too late.

He was a little bit of common sense in a world without reason. Head Office from Earth found him in the dust of the oxygenated air. The humans hadn't shot him at the end.

They didn't need to.

Unclean

The colored animals on Jeremy's shower curtain fell into the tub and swirled down the drain when he took a shower.

He could not keep on his plastic curtain the yellow lizard, the red snake, the blue crocodile or the green elephant. They nibbled on his toes as the chartreuse lion pranced within the hairs of his chest. The hot soapy water was like a surf to the creatures. Jeremy could hear their tiny screams of delight as they tore their colored hides from the vinyl sheet and reeled on the back of the spray.

The shower curtain came from a Swedish department store many years before. The stylized designs were bright and fun at first, but since then, the creatures had grown cloudy and grey with scum. Jeremy surmised they were slipping away from his lack of housekeeping, the layer of hard minerals from the bathroom water, and residue of the room deodorizers used over the years.

His toes were sensitive. He tried to step away from the colored animals as they churned down the drain, but he trod on a bar of soap and fell.

Jeremy hit his head on the side of the tub. The yellow lizard and blue crocodile turned red with Jeremy's blood. The chartreuse lion began to eat Jeremy's face.

When the EMS arrived, called by a concerned neighbor, the attendants first had to deal with the flood that poured onto the bathroom floor and soaked through the drywall into the suite next door.

"Where's the shower curtain?" The attendant scratched his head, after the mess was cleaned up. "I think there used to be a curtain."

"The guy's in the tub, the spray's full force, the drain's clogged with colored bits of plastic. Appears to me like he drowned." The female paramedic shivered as though the overhead vent blasted an icy wind.

"I never seen so much blood."

"He don't have a cat, does he? Looks like sharp bites. Or a small dog."

"You're right, Edgar."

"Something smaller than that. Like a small sharp backscratcher went at him."

"Poor guy." The female paramedic put her hand over Jeremy's eyes and closed them. "Looks as though his last glimpse of life terrified him. That's pure panic on his face."

"He wasn't much of a housekeeper, was he?" the attendant asked. "Take a gander at this room."

"It's filthy," the paramedic agreed. "I wonder how anyone can live like that?"

"I don't think he had pets. A good thing. Even animals would leave."

Awful Waffles

The mechanical chef couldn't cook but Richard thought his grandmother needed the company of such a handsome appliance, which he'd bought on sale from Robocom Inc. for a mere $150,000. Richard liked a bargain and suspected all along that the streamlined shining chef was faulty, but since his grandmother was in her nineties, Richard thought it wouldn't matter if her food was bad. He wanted to ingratiate himself with the old woman and spent her money to do so.

"You need the company, Grams," he explained, lighting a Havana cigar. "This way you won't have to go down to the cafeteria every day for meals. Marcus the Robot will prepare whatever you ask him to. He'll even go grocery shopping for you. How would you like that?"

Richard hoped for a speedy settlement of the will when his grandmother died, as certain she would soon, and a large part of her estate would be his if he played his pinochle right.

"What did you say, dear?" Grams asked, slipping on her Nikes. "I'll be jogging if you need me."

"Yes, by all means," Richard replied. "I was just telling you about Marcus here, the mechanical chef. I bought him for you so you won't have to go downstairs to the cafeteria with the old folks for meals anymore. It will make life easier for you. I hope he goes easy on the salt."

"Thank you. He looks like Justin Bieber now that Justin's all grown up. A sort of smooth and shiny Bieber, but handsome just the same. Does he sing?"

"I think so." Richard said.

"It doesn't matter then if he can't cook." Grams jogged out the door, down the stairs and left Richard alone with Marcus the Robot.

They stared at one another.

"Do you sing?" Richard asked. Marcus opened his mouth and began Irving Berlin's first song, *Marie from Sunny Italy*.

"Grams will like that. Let's see what's in her cupboards." Richard and Marcus opened doors and drawers, searching for ingredients. They found wild rice, quinoa, cans of stewed tomatoes, boxes of whole grain crackers, brie and mozzarella cheese, radishes, lettuce, milk and juice in the fridge, frozen vegetables, chicken and Tilapia fish in the freezer.

"Very full larder," Richard said. "You can make something great from this, Marcus. Let's surprise her."

"Where's the flour and sugar?" Marcus asked.

"Oh, you do talk. Well, they're here in canisters. I'm proud of Grams. She eats well."

"I make waffles."

"Can't you make anything else? It's dinner time."

"I make waffles."

Grams returned an hour later, panting, and tore off her Nikes. She sat on the couch and sipped a glass of wine while Marcus puttered about the kitchen. He emerged moments later with a magnificent waffle and homemade syrup.

"Very nice." Richard smiled and raised his eyebrows.

Turned out that waffles were all Marcus was good at. Chocolate waffles for breakfast with jam, blueberry waffles for lunch with whipped cream, whole grain and flax waffles for dinner with raspberry syrup.

Grams was delighted. Richard grew tired of waffles each time he came for dinner.

"Is that all you can make?" he asked the Robot one day.

"No," Marcus said. "I make roast chicken."

The chicken was pink inside and burned on the bottom. The potatoes were lumpy and hard. The chef forgot the salad. The fresh rolls were somehow soggy.

"Very disappointing," Richard said.

Marcus continued to make waffles and sang. He sang an aria from Aida. He sang classic rock 'n' roll. He sang Cole Porter songs, which Grams liked. Marcus was driving Richard over the line from neurotic to psychotic.

Richard began to visit less often. Grams never tired of waffles and songs. She began to thrive on the company of Marcus. Richard wondered if the old woman would ever stop jogging, stop the health consciousness, start pushing up sunflowers in the plot he'd paid for twenty years before. Richard was the only living relative. He had dreams of retiring early then dreams of traveling with senior groups, then he began to worry. Perhaps Marcus was good for Grams. Maybe Grams would outlive Richard. Grams seemed happy.

Richard tinkered with the machinery; reset the controls.

Marcus burned the waffles for the first time.

"Marcus," the grandmother chided. "What's wrong?"

"I don't know, miss," the robot said. "Something's changed. Maybe I make some beef bourguignon. I sing you aria from Nabucco."

"Song for Liberty? My favorite."

The Nikes were untouched that evening. Grams went to bed early and died in her sleep.

Richard sat in the barrister's office counting the grains of sand in the hourglass.

"It seems the beef bourguignon was spoiled," the attorney began. "You're not under suspicion, Richard, and a mechanical device can't be sued except under special circumstances."

"How awful," Richard said.

"But the will..." the attorney began.

"Yes?"

"She's left everything to Marcus, I'm afraid, Richard."

"Marcus? But he can't inherit. He's a robot."

"I'm afraid our laws have changed somewhat. A robot may indeed inherit an estate."

"Son of brown sugar."

"There's one thing. If a robot may inherit the estate, a robot may also be charged with murder. That's the special circumstance."

"What choices do I have?" Marcus asked the lawyer. He began to hum Song for Liberty.

"Give back the money or go to back to Robocom Inc. for refurbishing, I'm afraid."

"I go back for refurbishing," Marcus said. "It doesn't hurt."

Marcus lived in Gram's suite after that and entertained Richard. He burned the waffles every time he tried them, but made beautiful meatloaf, which Richard loved. Eventually Richard died of a heart attack at age sixty-two. He was overweight and smoked. Pity.

Marcus began to make waffles again. No one came to his home. The police broke in two years later and couldn't make their way past the waffles stacked from floor to ceiling—blueberry waffles, whole grain, apricot, buttermilk, flax, and other waffles Marcus had invented. Marcus was busy in the kitchen burning waffles when the constables seized him and took him back to Robocom Inc.

Cyclops

The giant eyeball washed up on the beach in Kitsilano early on the morning of April 8th. Jennifer found it sloshing about on the sand as the sun gilded the edges of the dawn during her morning run.

"It's a good thirty cm across," she muttered, backing away. Her companion, Trent, poked at the eyeball.

"The size of a soccer ball," he said. "There's a monster in the ocean."

"I don't want to touch it."

"We should bring it up to the marine biologists at UBC," Trent said.

"Maybe we should call the coast guard."

"Good idea. I wouldn't want to carry it."

A couple of children ran toward them. Their dark-eyed nanny stayed some length away. "Come back here!" she called. "From here, that thing looks dirty and dangerous."

"It's not," trilled the youngest girl. "It's a creature we know."

"Do you?" Jennifer touched the shining hair of the child. "Listen to your nanny. Don't go near it. It could be dangerous."

"The creature's dead," Trent said. "It's obviously from a monster."

"Monster," the eldest girl said. "Like our teacher told us in Greek tales at school. It's a Cyclops eye."

"That's it!" Jennifer said. "It's from the mythological giant that Odysseus blinded."

"Don't be silly." Trent shooed the children back to their nanny. The nanny smiled at Trent and Jennifer from a few paces away.

"The children know their stories," she said. Her warm brown face crinkled. "What an ugly eye."

"It's pretty," trilled the youngest child. "It looks like a ball."

"It's the size of a soccer ball," Trent repeated. "Want to play?"

"No-o-o." The girl shrieked and hid behind her nanny, who laughed.

Trent used his cell phone to call a local television station. A photographer and reporter arrived and police arranged for transport to marine scientists at UBC.

The reporter followed. "Is it from Mars?"

"No," the scientist replied, "it's the eyeball of a colossal squid, the largest eye known in the animal kingdom, now or ever. It's bioluminescent with a built-in headlight, and the other eye must be damaged or somewhere nearby. Fascinating."

In the ocean, on an island miles away, the Cyclops wept with an empty socket for an eye, and cursed Odysseus, who had blinded him.

Waiting for Nikolai

"The train is late."

"He will not be here." The artist soldier glances up from his painting, touching sierra oils to the outline of his captain, so noble and doomed with a vision of the past and a rucksack stuffed with souvenirs of the Great War.

Clouds of dense black smoke steam from the iron horse, chuffing into Petrograd. Soldiers in dun-colored wool huddle on the platform, this one standing out from the others. Tall like the Tsar.

The Great War is almost over. By the end of the war, the Russian empire will have ceased to exist.

The Battle continues, however, now between the old and the new, the aristocracy and the proletariat.... there are clashes in the streets between soldiers and peasants rioting for change. Boris Voskoboynikov, the standing captain in the high leather boots, represents the past.

Meanwhile, the painter captures his heroic image on canvas, the pivotal moment between history and a glorious future.

A brawny arm emerges from a portal of the train. The decorated ironwork slides back and Nikolai strides onto the platform, casting down his duffel bag next to the painter, and he squints at Boris, so huge and calm, standing there in the midst of the bustle of Russian soldiers.

The painter's brushstrokes are heavy and accented with the noble features of the soldier, casting in shadow and brown the crags of a face Nikolai knows well.

"I've been waiting for you, brother."

The painter flexes his icy fingers which clutch the thick brushes.

"I said you wouldn't come," Boris said.

"It was a long ride from the Front."

"They sent you back here to the capital, brother."

"I'm needed here. The garrison in the City is not enough to defend our Tsar."

"I have forces at my command. You too?" Boris Voskoboynikov stands tall like a monument to war.

"There's a lot of bustle here." Nikolai snaps his fingers. A soldier in a fur cap whips a rifle to his shoulder and stands at attention. Others form behind Boris. The painter claps his painting box to his back just as his thick crimson blood squirts onto the canvas. He collapses across the painted features he captured so recently, those of Boris Voskoboynikov, the noble captain of His Majesty's garrison here in Petrograd.

It is a short revolution, nothing like the October Revolution to come. Nikolai snaps the bayonet into place on his rifle and guts his brother.

Long Walk To Gadara

Day dawned as grey as the evening was before it, though the rain had stopped. Beyond the town of Gadara, a few miles away from the coast of the Sea of Galilee, the blue-grey mountains rose from a pearly mist. Early though it was, a large herd of swine were being driven with loud cries from their pens to feed on the roots and berries found on the slopes beside the tombs. Moving alongside the swineherds, helping with boyish enthusiasm, were two youths, Benjamin and Levi, the sons of the man who owned the herd. They often went to the fields or the hills with their father's men that they might better learn the management of their father's estates.

This morning, as usual, they avoided the immediate vicinity of the tombs, heeding their father's advice and their mother's warnings. Gulls flew screeching from the sea which lapped like sluggish molten metal in the dawn. A few fishing vessels were already casting off from the harbor, the fishermen's voices laconic and gentle, their movements deft. A leper's bell chimed in the distance.

Slowly the sun rose from the mists, gibbous and red. Benjamin, who was seated on the ground removing a pebble from his sandal, glanced with apprehension at the herd which rooted all around him. If a storm arose the swine would be all right. The herdsmen would have to seek shelter in the hut nearby, which had been built for that purpose. Fortunately the madman who lived in the hills seemed to prefer his cave, for the tombs were in caves. He and his leprous companions never crossed the slopes between the feeding grounds of the swine and the tombs where the outcasts made their homes. The madman's cries could be heard even now as he prowled, cutting himself with stones no doubt, feeding on yesterday's fish or a scrap of meat or bread which someone had left him. Benjamin grimaced with distaste and rose to join his brother not far away.

On the other side of the sea, at Capernaum on the coast, a prophet preached in parables to a multitude by the shore. They pressed so closely about him that he took to a small ship moored close to shore, and he and his disciples preached from the ship. Even so, the people on the shore pressed into the water. They waded out to touch the sides of the prophet's craft and touch his hand, or his garments, or the hands of his disciples. Many were healed and many more listened and turned away, pondering his words in their hearts. There were many, too, who rejected what he said.

He was said to be the King of the Jews, and a sorcerer, a healer, a prophet, and all along the shores of this sea and beyond, the people had heard of him and his powers. In the country of Decapolis, about the town of Gadara, the boy Benjamin had heard, and his brother Levi. They sometimes talked of the man Jesus and his miracles. So when that evening the prophet and his followers, in many little ships, sailed from Capernaum to cross the tiny sea, it was to a land wherein the seeds of his name had begun to stir. It was a name that even the madman of Gadara recognized when rumor had passed along the news of the possible departure of the prophet's ships from Capernaum to their shores.

The swine had been driven back to their pens. The sea was dismal and dark underneath a dreary sky, evening was grey with the threat of a storm and rain that had not yet fallen. The madman sat on the lip of his cave and faced the sea. The man seemed scarcely less soft nor of more substance than the rock upon which he sat. He too seemed made of earth, skin close to his bones, rolled in grime, lacking sanity so not quite human, yet not a beast either, without an animal's sure will to live its span in its appointed way. Mountain flowers and weeds were plaited in his hair and kept in place by mud, now dried. Dried blood, too, coated most of his face and body. He continued to cut himself with rocks, deriving a small pleasure from the sting of the reality of his flesh.

He lived from what nourishment the sea and the rocky hills about would provide. He stole fish and picked berries from amongst the tombs where he made his home. The madman ate what anyone gave him; anything to keep himself alive, and this he did with incredible energy and amazing strength for a man of such emaciated aspect and changeable mind.

He had the fury of a thousand devils when aroused and could break the strongest chains the men of Gadara put upon him. That's why they left him alone, to roam in the hills among the tombs beside the sea, and they let him steal what he could to keep himself alive. Sometimes they gave him sustenance from pity. His violence frightened them, but their religion forbade that they put him to death. Thus he had been banished to the tombs, he and others like him, from the haven of town where his kinsfolk still mourned him.

Crouched farther down the steep incline, behind a rock and some bushes, the two boys lay flat on their stomachs together and watched him. The madman couldn't have seen them. They whispered and shivered, and peered around the rock.

The old, wild ecstasy filled him suddenly. He jumped to his feet and roared at the sky, shaking his fist and clutching at his filthy garment with his other hand. His limbs jerked and flew about as though pulled and violated by a mad puppet master. The boys smirked.

"Whooo! Whaaaa!" The madman yelled and cavorted. Lightning zagged above his head and beyond him, silhouetting his form.

"Look at him, he's crazy, see what he's doing." The boys giggled and poked one another.

"Look at the crazy man, Levi. Father says he's crazy and could break our necks with the flat of his hand." The older boy, Benjamin, was very brave, very daring. He inched farther around the rock.

"We'd better get home," said the youngest, thinking of his mother, hearing her words of caution, thinking of her fear.

"Lie still," the oldest boy whispered, peering through the bushes, drawn by curiosity to a more venturesome position. The youngest followed, out of fear to be alone. They watched. The madman threw his arms and feet into the air, whirling and pounding and singing. The dance was an eerie one to see, the madman jerked about against a pallet of lowering sky, his feet in ragged sandals pounding faster and faster. The heavens in great thundering answering volumes of sound opened up. The earth was drenched and the sea beyond, until all was lost behind a curtain of rain and nothing more could be seen. The wind howled.

The boys rose to their feet together and ran laughing, half in terror, half in mirth, back to their home. Slipping and running and crowing, the eldest ahead, the youngest glancing back over his shoulder occasionally as he ran.

"The children *like* me," the madman muttered, his eyes as yellow as straw. A spirit burned within him, hotter than Hades. The demons drove him stumbling along the cliff-side, feet slipping in the mud along a path that threatened at any time to ooze its substance over the edge to the rocks below, and he with it. His fingers clutched and slipped at sodden leaves and branches by the way, until he was crawling and sliding on all fours, burning with fever. He slipped in the pelting rain, to the bottom of the hill and the entrance to his cave wherein he crawled. The madman coughed and covered up his body with a dirty blanket from the floor. He slept.

The storm had materialized miles away at sea as well. It struck suddenly, as was usual in that region, and would just as suddenly die. But the men in the ships which had left Capernaum were not at all sure they would not die with it. The winds were fierce and the rain was a curtain that would not allow them to see the other ships nor even one another's face an arm's length away. In the ship where Jesus lay asleep his disciples bailed water from both sides of the craft, with little effect. The sails, before they could take them down, were torn and ripped in a dozen places.

No one had foreseen winds of such intensity, nor that a storm would arise so suddenly at sea, so late in the evening. They should have been forewarned. Surely they would have been wise to have postponed their trip from the coast to Decapolis. All in a panic they cried to the God that was of Abraham. Many sat and wailed, others rowed frantically or bailed water as it came thundering over the sides of their ship. Some clambered, soaking wet, to the rear of the ship where their Lord slept, and they woke him.

Some would say the Lord was already awake, but he seemed unconcerned at the condition of the craft. The anxiety of his disciples seemed to fill him with amusement. He turned over as though to go back to sleep, for he was tired, but they persisted. In terror, although the wind drowned out most of their words, they besought him to arise, most of them bewailing that they had ever left the shores of Capernaum.

"O ye of little faith," he said finally, and stood up in the prow of the ship. He spoke to the wind and the seas. Tumult lashed his face. The storm roared about him, whipping his white garments about his muscular form. Then silence. The sea became calm. The wind blew no more. The waters ceased to pour from the sky, and the little craft was still.

So they arrived in the morning at the coast near Gadara, Jesus and his disciples, most rowing in the now calm waters. Many more men from Capernaum in little ships followed. Jesus lay in the hindermost part of the first ship, asleep once again. He had labored hard for many days sowing seeds amongst the multitudes, and he was tired. The sea and the land, too, shimmered like an opal, belying the storm of the night before; shimmered with blues and greens, milky with the mists of dawn and the promise of heat. Scarlet flowers clung to the rocky slopes of the hills before them as they approached the coast. The tombs amongst the cliffs looked black and cool. The sun rose huge and orange, sucking the moisture from the land and glimmering on the gentle sea that nudged the shore and lapped about the docks. The little ships drew near land and were still.

The madman of Gadara met them at the shore.

His disciples were awakening the Lord. They called him "Master." The madman heard this and fear detonated like a bomb the Hades that frothed inside his soul. He howled, picked a stone from the shore and flung it at the men who waded in the water by the ship's side, fastening it with ropes to the dock. The madman tore at his scanty clothes and cursed in a foreign tongue. He wept with anger. The stone he had thrown cracked against the Lord's ship.

He who lay in the back of the ship arose, and his face was stern. The madman drew back, alarmed. His hand held yet another stone. He dropped the hard object and faltered.

"Leave me alone, son of God," he cried. "What have I done to Thee?" And he turned, as though to run, but the prophet held him with a word and a motion of his hand.

"Jesus, son of Man," the madman pleaded, "do not torment me. My name is Legion. They say I'm many devils in one poor body, as you see. Leave me alone, as the men of Gadara leave me alone." He wept and tore his hair. His anger had turned once again to fear.

Jesus stepped from the ship to the water; walked away from the ships onto the slopes of the mountain. He took his place beside the madman. Nearby sat the boys Benjamin and Levi, who had witnessed the mad dance of the evening before. They were tending the herd of swine.

When they saw the madman weeping close to the prophet they, too, were afraid. The calm aspect of the white clothed man beside the madman stopped the boys from running. The many men debarking from small boats were comforting to behold for their numbers and their help if the need should arise. As the boys watched, the man they knew in their hearts was Jesus of Nazareth, called the Son of God, drew himself up like a blazing fire, and laid his hands on the madman's face. His eyes flashed and his garments shone. He threw up his arms to the sky and thundered in a mighty voice. The boys trembled and hid their eyes.

"Be gone in the name of God," Jesus cried, and as he said this the madman started and his eyes opened wide as though from a trance. But the swine that the boys attended gave a great squeal that could be heard as far away as the outskirts of Gadara, for there were almost two thousand of the beasts, and they all ran grunting and squealing down a steep hill to the sea. Most of the swine were crushed in their panic; drowned in the waters and dashed on the rocks. Those that did not immediately perish began to swim far out into the sea, and were drowned there. Not a beast remained on land.

The boys were appalled and the swineherds in utter confusion.

"Come with me, Levi!" Benjamin cried, and began to run from the shore back to their father's house. The swineherds, roused from their temporary immobility, followed and soon outdistanced the boys. They told their master, the man who owned the swine, and all his neighbors, and most of the townsfolk, what had happened, for most had heard the commotion and came running to find out the cause.

The boys' father was a rich man but the loss of two thousand swine was not to be taken lightly. When he heard the story he was incensed and determined to go to the seaside with most of the townspeople of Gadara and vicinity, and see for himself what had actually transpired.

The Gadarenes had heard of this Jesus, the miracle worker. Their journey to the shore was made with mixed emotions. What sort of man was this, who drove out devils with the sound of his voice in the name of God, and could destroy two thousand swine with a gesture of his hands? People said he drove out devils wherever he preached. Such devils were better left alone, they believed, lest they loose themselves upon the town and innocent people. Perhaps the prophet drove out devils with a devil.

The people of Gadara, after a while, then came upon Jesus and his followers and the madman sitting in their midst. The madman was clean and clothed in fresh garments. He was conversing in quiet tones with the disciples Matthew and Mark, and the Christ, who gazed every now and then at the quiet hills. Another man, who also lived in the tombs, stood silently some distance back, his wonderment a cloak upon him. No word had been spoken in his direction yet he felt a great peace. The men at the seaside stirred impatiently and many more were still in their ships, which rocked and waited in the bay. The men of Gadara confronted them.

"I pray you, Lord, depart from our shores," another man begged, for he was superstitious and wanted none of devils or those who cast them out. He who had been mad sat, as before, quietly on the ground. Benjamin and Levi, who had followed their father, cast many an apprehensive look at the former madman, but he did not stir or return their glances.

"Let the man speak for himself," Jesus said quietly, but the poor wretch shook his head. He directed his gaze at the ground once more. No one spoke. The disciple Simon Peter shuffled his feet in the rocky soil. The prophet bade him be still.

"We beseech you," one of the Gadarenes said. Some wept in fear and supplication. The man who had owned the swine walked up to the ridge of the hill and gazed into the sea. Many swine still bobbed amongst the rocks, and others squealed and gurgled far out from the shore. Most had sunk beneath the waves and were lost from sight, hundreds upon hundreds of them. Others followed as their owner watched; struggled, foaming and frothing, far out from shore and perished. The wealthy landlord stood at the top of the cliff and shook his fist at Jesus, tried to intercept the pigs racing past him, but was unsuccessful. Tears ran down his cheeks. Finally, he shrugged their shoulders and stared, next turned on a worn sandal and spread his arms in supplication to the open sky, to his God, who had allowed this.

As he made his way down the hill again to the people waiting at the harbor, the boys' father saw that the followers of Jesus had put themselves back into their crafts and were pushing off from shore. Jesus himself was the last to leave. He was being hindered in his departure by the man who had been mad, who clutched at his sleeve and entreated that he might go back to Capernaum with Jesus and the others, for there was no place for him here. But the Lord was firm. He spoke quietly but sternly to the man. The healed man let go of the

Lord's sleeve and stepped back. The last ship left the harbor at the request of the terrified townspeople.

The people of Gadara turned back to the town, back to their farms and their trades, and left the seashore empty of all but the waves, the gulls and the persistent sound of a leper's bell in the hills. The man who was healed of his madness stood silently in the midst of this emptiness. He was alone, and his pity stirred within him. The answering stir from the sea was a radiance of mind and soul.

He took his staff then, and bade in himself goodbye to the tombs, the hills and the sea. The long walk back to Gadara filled his heart with joy. He was joined at a distance by another figure, limping on its staff, shuffling from the hills that had been its prison and its haven. Now a new life began for all, the madman and his distant companions, for the hills were suddenly alive with ragged figures.

One by one, hesitantly, the townspeople welcomed them home. Cleansed and free, the madman of Gadara was no longer alone. His mother met him at the gate.

Years later, the tomb yawned deep and black around him as they laid him in his shrouds, placed his body on the mat of straw, and rolled the heavy stone in place. He was home again.

Matters about Monty

The only thing worse than hanging out with Monty was knowing he'd rather be with someone else, someone more popular, more attractive, but knowing he'd never have a chance with a girl like that. Knowing he was stuck with *me*.

Prim tagged along with us after school and the convo turned desultory. It's hard to be cool when your little sister follows after you like a basset hound that's lost the scent. Trouble is, I love little Prim and it's hard to blow her off when you love your little sis like that, even though she's a pain in the teakettle most days, and you know she's a spy. My mom put her up to it, spying on Monty and me. Not that Monty was hot, you see, but Mom didn't know a hot boy as opposed to something as tame as the Ottawa Arts Review.

I thought we needed to solve this particular issue fast. As we turned up our street, which was at the end of a cul de sac in sort of a blind alley, I gave Prim a little shove toward the door where Mom waited, cookies in hand, grabbed Monty's arm and bolted toward the open spaces at the other end of Dean Street. He was breathless and continued to hold my hand until, panting, we dropped to our butts where Dean Street intersected Tyson Boulevard, out of sight of our house.

"What'd you do that for?" Monty's face was red with zits and exertion. His dirty blond hair fell in his eyes and he flicked it up with his thumb.

"I felt like it." I fiddled with the buttons on my cardigan. "She's a spy. Like the Three Wise Men." Monty's hand was hot on my jeans. I sat huddled in the snow at the T intersection.

The street was quiet.

"Let's go, sea donkey." My cell phone crowed like a rooster. It was how I knew it was mine. Who'd be calling me? I only had one friend, plus Monty, and my friend Deirdre would text.

Monty's fingers fumbled with the folds of my sweater.

"Oh, no, you don't. Hello? No, I didn't mean you, Dad. I meant... I'm at the library." *Yes, that's it. Lie to your dad again. Lie, lie, lie, lie, lie.*

"It was a sudden decision. No, Prim's perfectly all right at home. I don't need her here with me, Dad. No, tell Mom I'm all right. Yes, Monty's here with me. Yes, Dad. Good-bye."

Monty's here with me. I'm all right.

My sweater pulled up over my stomach and his sweaty hands pulled on the layers of clothes.

"That's enough, dude. I mean it." In spite of myself, I felt a warm flush that began where his hands covered mine. He pushed me back into the snow. His breath smelled like peppermints. His body exuded heat and a sort of animal smell that was not unappealing. I grabbed his hand and bent his fingers back. I heard a snap and he gasped and sat up.

"I told you."

Prim found us ten minutes later. "Are you and Monty hooking up?" she asked. "Mom and Dad had a horrible fight about you."

"No," I said. "We're not hooking up. You're wrong, Prim. It's just that... we have nobody else." Monty was walking away.

"That's sick," he said. The strains of Taylor Swift floated through the dark streets. A nervous fusillade of giggles tore through me and I sat on the street and laughed. It's just that we were two losers, and I was stuck with *him*.

I got up and we started back to our home, Prim and I. Mom met us at the door with cookies. I would text Deirdre tonight. It was going to be all right.

Ghoul Bite, Sweet Prince

Bram Stoker's stomach lurched with blood hunger. He wanted to enjoy himself on this little European holiday and London seemed a good place to start. Bram tried the Eye but it was too high and he was alone in a cool glass cubicle—no warm necks to suck. He streaked across the Tower Bridge after a bobby, wearing his Converses, but Englishmen don't like the naked truth and Bram escaped **jail** by a hair. He found the bloodlines of an old aristocracy in the Palace of Westminster, Buckingham Palace, and was closer to his goal. He dined that night in a gin palace beneath the Brasserie Knightsbridge in Aldwych. After, as he leaned vomiting from the Millennium Bridge, he met Prince Harry Locatelli. Bingo!

Or as his English host commented, "Bloody good, Bram." Blood interested Bram in more than a clinical sense. It was his lifeline and tonight he wouldn't need to break into a blood bank. Prince Harry's fluent Italian and ginger-haired good looks set a fire in Bram's soul.

"Join me?" he leered, breaking a bit of rusk into a flaçon of white wine. Flames crackled in a corner hearth and threw shadows across his gaunt grey face. Prince Harry's home was exquisite, and they were alone in the sitting room.

"It's the Host, isn't it?" Harry said, sucking on a sop of Dutch toast. "So appropriate for a vampire."

Bram preened. "You know me, then?"

"Everyone knows Bram Stoker."

"Even in England? I had hoped to escape notoriety."

"My father was Italian, you know, old fellow. Full of erotic stories."

"Ah. Cosmopolitan." Bram noticed the fine blue veins on Harry's wrist. Mmmm. "But erotic, you say? Surely you don't think…"

"I do." Harry sipped on his Chardonnay. "Nothing more erotic than an open mouth leading down to the jugular."

"What?" Bram may have made a mistake here. He gathered his wool coat around his thin shoulders, too thin, too long without a proper meal…

Harry pounced, pinning Bram against a Klimt painting that hung on the brocade walls.

"I was looking for you tonight," Harry snarled, and teeth like knives slashed at Bram's throat as a silver cross lacerated his chest. "On the bridge."

Bram scrabbled onto the marble floor, clenching Harry's ankle with ancient and dirty nails. Harry screamed.

Soon the contest solidified into a spectacle of *film noir*. The Klimt was crushed beneath the fighting men. Darkness seeped through stained glass windows into every corner of the room as they struggled; blood and hair and dirt defiled the fine carpets and mottled the marble to mirror Hell.

Thrown to scorch in the flare of the grate, Bram escaped to the hallway.

"Going somewhere, boys?" asked Harry's mother, and flung open the mahogany door. She smiled, revealing incisors like sharpened bone. Bram screamed and felt his throat crush beneath her soft insistent mouth.

* * *

Midnight and all was still. Bram rose from a crouch on the marble floor, flowing with blue-red blood, and staggered out the palatial side door.

As he reached the street, a pale hand grasped his ankle and pulled him back into Clarence House.

It's the Bees' Knees

from *SPACEHIVE*

My daughter is immune to Bee stings like I am. She will never grow old. Jay Anderson's immunity to Bee stings had been instrumental in developing a serum which killed the vicious alien Wasps and presented humanity with virtual immortality.

Jay glanced at his mother sipping tea in the other room, her face older but still beautiful. She was allergic to the antidote, made of alien Bee venom and his father's chemicals, and so his parents would age while the rest of Earth remained young and disease-free. His father had chosen not to take the serum as well, and grow old along with his wife.

Nine months before. On the horizon the starship balanced on a column of electromagnetic energy and air, hesitated, then purred into space. Jay stood with his wife and his friend, Aadab Ali, watching the small oval collapse upon itself and disappear into the stratosphere. His parents stood beside him. The young alien Bee nurse from the Rangoon hive lounged on the side of the hill beneath them, fanning herself with her translucent wings. She had chosen to stay. A smattering of human scientists and engineers left on Earth stared upward.

"This is only the first starship," they assured Jay. "This was the prototype. Others to follow; humanity is going to the stars, using alien technology, and this the first. In two years they'll be back. Our friendly

Bees are anxious to go home, and we must confront our Wasp attackers on their own ground, make sure this doesn't happen again."

Jay had been assured the pilots would get his human friends safely back to Earth, with the assistance of the computer-assisted mission control systems which would be in constant communication with the ship when it was out of hyperspace. As a precaution, two young engineers on board had been trained as emergency interim pilots if necessary. Hopefully emergency measures wouldn't be necessary.

This was the first starship to launch without exploding on acceleration into the stratosphere. No one knew the first ship carrying the Wasps home had been tampered with. Almost everyone assumed the technology had been faulty. All vicious alien Wasps had been killed and the human pilots escaped in sleek Air scooters.

No harm done. Jay's long golden hair fluttered across his wife's face. Aadab knew Jay's secret, the murder of the Death Watch, the escape Pod a means of last resort for his friendly Bees and the human pilots.

"Where's Beatrice?" Jay asked of their precocious young daughter, a strange child like an ancient fairy changeling.

"She chose not to come with us today. She's sulking, I think, because she wasn't allowed on board."

"Of course not. It's not possible to have a child on a mission like this."

Aadab cleared his throat. "Our new computer programs built into the starship will take Earth's population to the giant curve of the cosmos and back. The Japanese technology is great, and there's been no pressure to finish on a particular date."

"Only the pressure of the call home for the friendly Bees who want to leave Earth, and an appetite for adventure ever present in man." Jay's wife squeezed her husband's hand. She had been instrumental in convincing him not to volunteer.

"They'll be all right," his wife said. "Our soldiers and pilots will be back in less than two years, without our apian friends. Sad we have to leave them. They helped us so much since the War they lost."

The ocean lapped the beach not far from the hill on which they stood. His wife shifted her weight. "I think we can go now," she said. "Beatrice will be anxious for news."

A stereocam held by a Roboporter whirred next to them, videotaping the small crowd which had gathered to see the space travelers on their way. The pink flag of the United Federation of Nations (UFON) fluttered under a melting sun that morning.

"Our Earth, a global village after all. No more divisions of country and race and artificial symbols such as national flags. I think that pink rag is a mistake."

"Still, the UFON needs a symbol," Aadab said.

The white star and flame were emblazoned on the rose-colored silk and whipped in the hot wind like butterflies, or happiness that landed lightly on one's hand unsought.

Beside them, the Secretary from Old Russia stood watching the sky until the oval form of the ship disappeared into infinity. The pilots had turned on the hyperdrive; there was a lavender flame high near the sun and then a trail of smoke.

Someone watched the brilliant trail from where she stood beneath a Geiger tree. Her mouth drooped a bit at one side and she wiped a bit of spittle from her lips with a pink cloth.

It looks like a shooting star. Beatrice beneath the Geiger tree. She would watch by herself and then back to their little house in the jungle on the coast of Burma. She'd pick edible mushrooms, mangoes and breadfruit later today for their meal, then watch the news holograms before going to bed. She was sure everything would be all right.

Her parents had said no to her request to accompany the friendly Bees into space. *Too young; too frail.*

"Goodbye, brave soldiers," she whispered, and climbed into her air scooter. "Goodbye, Bees. Break a leg, sweethearts."

The scooter lifted into the cobalt sky toward home.

It's The Bees' Knees 2

A sequel note to SpaceHive

On board the starship shot from Earth's gravity, the next star system and then the next flashed by, and then they went into hyperdrive again, the computers at the command center silent until they flashed out the other end—they were there! The antigravity engines screamed as the brakes were applied, the triple moons shot past them, and they hovered to a halt above the night side of an alien world. The giant alien Bees on board buzzed with delight. Home at last!

The Earth soldiers and pilots thought there could be Death Wasps here, waiting for them. A corporal peered into the controls of the aliens' War Machine they had refurbished.

"They'll have War Machines, too," his captain cautioned. "Maybe more powerful."

"Maybe, Sir. Maybe not."

The captain raised his voice and sensitive microchips amplified it throughout the ship. "Everybody up. We're here!"

He felt his youth pouring back into his limbs, and it wasn't the effects of the recent protein spray injection either. They were rejuvenated by the serum Jay had helped discover, and it was plentiful on this trip. The captain peered out the portholes onto the moonlit scene below. A small craft rocketed toward them from the mysterious planet ground.

"I think we've got company," he said.

"Prepare to blast them out of the sky," the captain said. The Bees crowded around the command center.

"Don't do that, Earthling. Those are our hives, our people."

Several soldiers hovered at the controls of the War Machine, the Death Rays, ready to destroy the small craft, ready to incinerate the sudden activity on the ground below, seen through infrared lenses.

"We're just as bad as they are, Corporal," the captain said. "This little craft isn't going to hurt us. Prepare to take it aboard."

"Okay. Auto ports open."

"Receive."

The alien Pod was aboard.

It's The Bees' Knees 3

A note on SpaceHive and the Bees

The Earth pilots hovered their craft beneath the triple moons, the beautiful planet below mysterious and blue in the moonlight. Three friendly Bees, ready to translate, stood near the humans in their starship. The silver alien Pod that shivered in the docks looked familiar but was sleeker, the lines more streamlined, a bit larger than the Pods on earth. Many years had passed since the original Wasp emigration from this alien planet. Their technology, too, had moved on and now what would Earth be faced with, were these aliens still hostile?

The lovely planet of Atlantis, and the legend of Merlin, which all Earth now knew, since the ghastly Invasion.

A prequel to SpaceHive

The aliens' home was a fertile planet on the rim of the Milky Way galaxy, abounding with nectar and pollen, trees laden with sweet rotting fruit, flowers scattering their petals, stamens and pistils open to the zephyr-like winds of eternal summer, and small rivers and brooks in hundreds of valleys, undulating with silver cascading splashes and ripples from springs high in the pristine snow-capped mountains.

No enemies existed but the pressure of population itself.

Weeks before the invasion left their planet, the friendly worker Bees huddled over their fires many a damp night. Other bodies were pressed about them. No one danced, no one sang, no one flew or played the drums.

"It's said we come originally from a luscious planet named Mars, in the same solar system," an older Bee buzzed. "When we used up its resources we emigrated long ago, not to Earth, but to a companion planet closer to the sun, and were happy there, until the eruption of volcanoes and our own greed destroyed the land."

"Our ancestors sent a probe ship to Earth but were repulsed by dreadful magic and science beyond our understanding at the time. Our ancestor Zummershackle invented the Eternity Drive, which took us out of the star system of our birth into the edge of the galaxy, where we lived and prospered on numerous planets until to this day only Earth is left that's suitable to be populated."

"Our new home," a young Bee said.

"The Eternity Drive still exists, hidden in the Hollow Hills near the Death Watch and their huge soldiers, under the direct command of the Queen herself."

The Wasps of the Death Watch were striped black and yellow, and towered nine feet tall, their fuzz tipped with poison and their spikes instant and deadly. The workers feared the Death Watch through their long days and nights of bipping and bopping about the flower fields and orchards of their planet with the triple moons. All were aware of the Wasps' ominous presence, but none knew their necessity.

The Queen knew the Wasps guarded the Eternity Drive, an engine so powerful and a ship so huge it could transport half a planet of beings at a time, with little effort, to their new home in the silent reaches of black space, and bring them to a foreign shore with provisions for all, and the overwhelming Imperative due only to population constraints on their old beloved planet: colonize or die.

Earth waited as it had since the time of Merlin and Atlantis, and the original Invasion from Mars when the apians were neighbors in space. The leader of the Death Watch smiled.

It was time.

It's The Bees' Knees 4

Sequel to the families in SpaceHive

After the Battle of India twelve years ago, a war to the death with the giant alien Wasps, Jay moved to Burma with his young wife, Maria, and daughter, Beatrice. His lovely munchkin was born after the alien Bee wars and aptly named.

"I want a green gummygator, Dad."

Green gummygators were her favorite candy in all the world. They were also Jay's favorite candy when he had been a 13-year-old boy kidnapped and held for many months in the abdomen of the alien ship *SpaceHive*.

"I understand," Jay said. "A green one. Sticky is best."

He speared a hand into the pocket of his white and blue *kurta* and brought out a small moist bag of candy. "The color makes all the difference."

"Ask for a red one," his friend Aadab Ali suggested.

Jay snorted. He didn't have a red gummygator.

Beatrice wailed. "I want a *red* one."

"Like blood." Aadab Ali winked. Beatrice considered this and wailed again.

"I want one like *blood*. Like Uncle Aadab said." The little autocrat spread her fingers. "I want to feed the zombits at the zoo. They like gummygators, too."

"Please, Mom, can we go to the Zoo?" Beatrice turned her attention to another authority, sitting in the breezeway of the open deck, overlooking the Hanging Gardens of Burma which Jay and Aadab had created for the little family's enjoyment.

A month before, the monsoons had soaked the family on hikes to the far side of their little village. Rain for four months of the year and the only moderate temps were now, between November and February before the heat waves started. They lived on the coast, though, where the temperatures were cooler and more moderate. Jay's cotton shirt or *kurta* fluttered in the breeze that made its way into their garden from the Bay of Bengal. He had chosen to live in Myanmar, or Burma as it was known before the Change. *Forty degrees Celsius and heavy seasonal rains are a small price to pay for living in Paradise,* Jay thought.

Jay and his family were a few amongst many North Americans relocated to the new Myanmar after radioactivity destroyed most of their home continent. Not much was left of humanity. Those humans who survived the alien wars carved friendships with the friendly huge Bees who had helped defeat the vicious wasp General Vard twelve years previously.

"Let's go to the Zoo and see the zombits then," Maria said.

"How come zombits have *two* hairy heads, Daddy?" Beatrice settled into the driver's seat of the family's airpod. The controls were fortunately simple. Beatrice *would* drive. Scary thought, but she insisted.

"It happened after the Change, Bea. The bombs the Earth generals dropped on Canada's southwest spewed poison that killed and modified all living things on the planet after a while. Including what we now call zombits."

"Why did they do that?" The airpod jerked into the air and whirred above the village. Jay put out a hand to steady his daughter's grip on the levers.

"They tried to bomb the alien spaceship *SpaceHive*, which had settled on a mountain in Canada."

"That was pretty stupid. Could I have a blue gummygator, please?"

"All right. I ate the green ones."

"*Daddy!*" She wailed again. Maria began to braid Beatrice's hair from behind. Aadab popped some honeycomb into his mouth and chewed.

"I see the walls," Beatrice said, pulling away from her mother's hands.

Her father smiled. "Yes, there's the zoo and the zombit enclosure."

The airpod settled on the grass outside the zoo. Beatrice scrambled to be first to the gates.

"Four, please," Jay said. There was no charge but they did need tickets for a head count. Nothing in this new world cost anything. Everything was free. Humanity huddled alone on the Asian subcontinent where all their needs (and wants) were taken care of by the new technology introduced well before the Battle of India with the alien Wasps, and a new world government.

"They used to be called honey bears but now they're not bears anymore. We can't call them what we used to call them in the olden days," Jay commented. "It's like their DNA has changed and that's why our garden is such a hallelujah of color, too, new colors, Bea, new plants and animals."

"Is that why you and Mommy have only two arms?" Beatrice asked.

"No, darling, that's different. Mommy and I were born before the Change. We still have our original genes and our ancestors looked like this, too."

"I think you look funny."

Beatrice stared with her one large eye through the bars at the zombits in the grassy enclosure.

The starship *SpaceHive* was a memory, hanging like honeycombs in the night sky.

Apocalypse

"I want you both to know I love you very much." The man sat hunched beside his sister and mother, with the news of the terminal illness which would take his life within a few weeks.

"We were made for each other," the robot said, and spread its arms. Steven Robert Wild stepped into the void between them, full of stars and darkness—he took a breath then did not take another, and was gone.

Somewhere in the darkness his father waited, dead for all these years, forty-one of them, long and difficult years for Steve without a father. Difficult years for Steve, whose mother in the past was an alcoholic and mentally ill, and whose stepfather abused him emotionally and physically. Joy eventually bubbled from high school friends, work friends, school, work, play, and family. He loved to sit in his boxers after work, and cocoon. He loved robots, video games, and reading.

The robot was a kindly automaton, waiting for the crossover between worlds. Its eyes glowed in the night outside the open curtains where Steve lay in pain, the cancer snaking throughout his entire body from its original source.

Kindlier than the world, the void opened to the 44-year-old gentle man—a gentle giant, the boy whom his mother and sister remembered and loved. He slipped away into the waiting abyss.

His sister waited with him those brief months, weeks, and days for the last day of summer; Steve waited, too. The fall equinox of 2012 closed on a light snuffed out and a little bit of love gone from the world.

The apocalypse had come.

Wild Honey

You came to Snake Creek because you were desperate for a teaching job, but you stayed for love of a dusty farm boy with forearms like oaks. His name was Riggs.

When you finished Elementary Education at UBC and finally got your teaching certificate, the best schools were already taken, so you packed up your few belongings and headed for the Peace River country. The year was 1952 and Louis St. Laurent was Prime Minister—we were just six years out of WWII and a year into another war already. Your older brother was with the Princess Pats regiment, fighting in Korea, and you were determined to show your independence, too, in your own way.

"Patricia Jean," your mother said, and smacked the risen bread dough with the heel of her hand. "Patricia Jean, you've always had a stubborn streak. Your father and I can tell you have your heart set on leaving, though. Truth be told, I don't blame you." Your mother wiped her hands on the soiled apron that hung like dead sewn leaves from her bony frame. She lowered her voice. "I never told you this, Patricia, but I always hankered for an education, too. I married your father right out of Grade Twelve and never regretted it but once, when I saw those spires on the College there and realized I'd never walk through those gates on my own and collect a diploma of higher education. It was up to my daughter to do that."

"Thanks, Mom. I did the best I could for myself. It was either that or marry Henry Parker."

"You could have done worse than that."

"I didn't, though."

"I'm lonely already," your mother said.

"You'll have my brothers here."

The bread dough took a pounding. Finally satisfied, your mother covered it with a clean white linen towel and set it on the sideboard to rise again. She sighed, apparently thinking deep thoughts that you could never know.

"A daughter," she said. "A daughter is special."

It didn't take you long to pack into your vintage car a carpetbag, several boxes of books, a few articles of good clothing for the first semester of school, and your bedding and cooking supplies.

"Goodbye, Pat." Your youngest brother extended a grubby hand. "Want a jaw breaker? I bought one just for you."

"No, thanks, Bruce," and you kissed the top of his auburn head, kissed your parents goodbye, even your grim father's face, and then you wiped your moist eyes and climbed back into the Mini Minor. The old red car leaned to one side while all four thin tires threatened to go their separate ways down the potholed street and into the August heat. I was there with you, a silent partner who felt your sorrow and excitement mixed like that all together. You wished the Mini had a radio so you could hear the news of the Korean War and where your older brother must be stationed in Seoul, 5,000 miles away from Burnaby.

Four days later you and your baggage were in Snake Creek, shaking hands with the neighbors who lived across the dusty road from the little schoolhouse, climbing their rickety stairs to your room on the second floor, splashing your face with cool water from a bucket to rinse away the dirt of the road.

I sat in a corner and watched, silent and invisible as the ghosts that haunt the Vogue Theatre back home.

When you flew down the stairs that night at the sound of the dinner gong, you little knew the rest of your life was destined to the farmhand

Wild Honey

introduced as Riggs, thumbs hooked in the pockets of his tight jeans, a belt buckle the size of Texas shining dully over taut stomach muscles. He'd thrown his shirt casually across his broad shoulders and his chest hairs were a carpet of gold that glistened like oil while his chest tapered to a slim waist.

You halted at the bottom of the stairs and held out your hand.

"The new teacher," Riggs said, and strode around the table to take your hand in both of his tanned ham hocks of sinew and flesh.

He was bold, and you didn't like that. Later, he seemed shy, a mixture of enigmatic traits. The landlords sat you next to him at the dinner table then and until you tumbled into love with him.

Six months later you were married and introduced to the community as Mr. and Mrs. Keith Riggs. You had to quit your job; teachers weren't allowed to be married in those days in that area. You were happy to call your mother on the party line and invite her to the bridal shower, after you and Riggs were hitched, of course. Your mother was speechless and crying, your father blustered, "Who is this guy?" and your younger brother asked, "Does this mean I can have your room?"

Riggs had a few acres of land on a place just miles from Snake Creek, on the southwest corner of his daddy's four sections. He lived in a trailer and farmed himself out as a helper during harvest season. For a wedding gift his daddy gave you and Riggs a half section of prime land, with an Angus bull and six heifers, one a good milker, and a forest out back of the trailer. Neighbors got together and quickly raised a two-storey plank house for you and your new husband. Riggs raised Arabian horses, he'd had a dozen of them on his few acres. He traded one for a used International tractor and a good roping pony.

You would have a ranch in your future together, you and the handsome farm boy with brown hair and hazel eyes, eyes that smoldered when they looked at you, Patty, and backbreaking work formed his arms and legs like muscles on a bull. Nights otherwise were spent hunched over maps and plans, bank statements and debit vouchers, textbooks on agriculture, samples of grain that sprouted on windowsills in the kitchen, you with your treadle Singer sewing machine clacking all afternoon, busy with curtains and sheets and tea towels and a new dress; shirts for Riggs.

Baby clothes.

Yes, there was a family, while you chafed at motherhood. A little boy Bob and later, little Jeannie, who died in her crib one summer afternoon. A precious baby love snuffed out, and that's when your husband became more silent and unapproachable, and that was when you discovered the bees in the forest.

They flew to the bole of the most ancient of pines in the forest just a quarter mile from your farmhouse. You followed them the day that Jeannie was buried. When you came home you changed your black dress with trembling fingers. Your eyes were dry—no more tears allowed to trickle in smudged tracks down your pale cheeks. Riggs changed from the navy suit that was too small across the shoulders, into his GWGs and plaid shirt, and lumbered toward the stables to groom his favorite mares over and over... and over... he groomed the mares until their coats shone, then he disappeared, as he would thereafter, for days at a time, and came back smelling of whisky.

But the bees. You discovered them on their secret path, just far enough from the wild roses and the honeysuckle to make it to the hole in the ancient tree. To make honey for the hive, to feed the Queen who routinely killed her daughters. You discovered the bees and their wild honey there in the secret dark moss dankness of the forest behind your no longer welcoming house and the stranger you had married.

While the honeybees droned and scattered about their stash of succulent sweet dripping hive, you dashed your hands into the pot of honeycomb and came out, all covered with bees and wax, and *you weren't stung, Patty.*

Carefully, with hands that knew how to love, you scooped the bees from their treasure and tasted it. Eyes closed and chin tilted to the sun above the dappled leaves, you savored the sweetness and the guilt of a stolen joy.

Back at the farmhouse, your son looked for his father and found him, face down in a fragrant prickly haystack, drunk.

You knew that Bob needed you and so, reluctantly, you bore the stolen treasure in both hands to the kitchen. You scooped the goodness from the octagonal cells where still moved the sleepy bees who wouldn't harm you or your son. Your husband stumbled home and you held out your sticky arms and cried together, eyes streaming on each other's shoulders. Bob watched and waited for his turn, his small arms reaching out to touch his father's waist, and Riggs enveloped him and you in a bear hug.

The honeycomb lay forgotten on the dripping crawling counter. Only then was the loss mourned truly, the family of three huddled together, wept and swayed on the dry grey boards of the floor.

In the long cool afternoons of the autumn, you swept like a summer breeze into the forest, to the hole in the old pine, to the treasures held by bees. To the wild honey. Others before you had done as much; it was now a new millennium, the Korean War long over, but more wars spilled the blood of youths. No longer an idyllic time as life had been in 1952 for white Protestant people who were not much different from their white Protestant neighbors. Your older brother came back unscathed from Seoul. He now worked in a diamond mine in Yellowknife, your younger brother became an engineer at Datek Industries. Your father died of a stroke in 1956.

Your mother lived alone in the big house on Hastings Street in Burnaby. You visited her every spring because spring in Vancouver is the most beautiful of seasons, and you missed her. Then she, too, died and the house on Hastings Street was sold.

Always the seasons of hard work on the farm, and Bob helping his father covered up for the many absences and smell of whisky. Your son grew tall like his father. One grey day he left home for the big cities when he no longer could tolerate the tension. Riggs and you didn't weep, but a bit of love again was gone from your lives. You had one child, and he left an empty chair at the dinner table. Riggs and you worked harder to make up for the lack of Bob's strong arms on the farm. He visited on holidays and on your birthday.

The wild honey was harvested every fall. You came there the last time in September of 2017, an old woman who still moved briskly, and you saw the many women who had gathered the wild honey before you. They were sleeping in the meadow behind the pines, dozens of them, from the gentle brown Cree girls to the pioneer women with bustles and bows and curls.

There was someone else, too, as you thrust your hands for the last time into the mass of sticky sweetness. Riggs inexplicably came up behind you, his hands around your still tiny waist.

He had followed you all these years, silent and invisible, like me, your sister who died in her crib before you were born—your older sister, invisible as the ghosts in Central Park in Burnaby.

We are there in the meadow, the young girls, amongst the many women who gathered wild honey before you. We welcome you here for the last time.

Your husband releases you. Through the ether I hear him wail, before we take you home.

Welcome home, sweetheart. You've been a long time away and we've missed you.

Music Of The Spheres

The philosopher pulled on his ill-groomed beard and bent over his quill and paper. The candle smoked on his desk. Pythagoras and, in turn, Plato had proposed what the philosopher was proposing, through centuries of oral tradition, the Music of the Spheres produced by the planets in proportion to their distance from the Earth, and heard by those dying, in exquisite harmony.

The philosopher had never heard the tones of the Cosmic Muse produced by the magic of mathematics or the stretching of interplanetary distances. He relied on the teachings of the Pythagoreans and the Roman statesman and mathematician Boethius, who believed in the harmony of all things. He believed that on the point of death, he would at last hear the rarified and exquisite tones.

Millennia later, in the 21st century, humanity was to rediscover *Musica Mundana*, or the Music of the Spheres, and begin again to treat dis-ease with music.

Ham radio operators in the 20th century would bounce their signals off meteorite trailers and hear 'whistlers' from these trailers to determine the location.

"*Researchers from the Electric and Magnetic Field Instrument Suite and Integrated Science (EMFISIS) team at the University of Iowa have released a new recording of an intriguing and well-known phenomenon known as "chorus," made on Sept. 5, 2012. The Waves tri-axial search coil magnetometer and receiver of EMFISIS captured several notable peak* radio wave events in the magnetosphere that surrounds the Earth. The radio waves, which are at frequencies that are audible to the human ear, are emitted by the energetic particles in the Earth's magnetosphere.

"People have known about chorus for decades," says EMFISIS principal investigator Craig Kletzing, of the University of Iowa. "Radio receivers are used to pick it up, and it sounds a lot like birds chirping. It was often more easily picked up in the mornings, which along with the chirping sound is why it's sometimes referred to as 'dawn chorus'."

Highly Allocthonous wrote, 'The Sounds of Earth's Magnetosphere, at frequencies directly audible to humans!'[1] The Earth rolled on and hummed and chirped, and the seven other planets chirped on their own lengths of harmonic sound.

The dying man heard it, and entered the Light.

The philosopher smiled in his grave as the universal concert sang.[1]

http://climatecrocks.com/2012/09/18/music-of-the-spheres-the-sounds-of-earths-magnetosphere/

---

1. Credit: University of Iowa.

About The Author

Kenna McKinnon is the author of *SpaceHive*, a middle grade sci-fi/fantasy novel; *BIGFOOT BOY: Lost on Earth*, published by Mockingbird Lane Press, a traditional small press. A children's chapter book, *Benjamin & Rumblechum*, was published by Mockingbird Lane Press in January 2015. *The Insanity Machine*, a self-published memoir with co-author Austin Mardon, PhD, CM; and *DISCOVERY – A Collection of Poetry*, were released by CreateSpace in 2012. Her books are available in eBook and paperback worldwide on Amazon, Smashwords, Barnes & Noble, etc., and in selected bookstores and public libraries.

Her interests / hobbies include fitness and health, volunteering, reading, writing, learning French, and walking. She lives in a high-rise bachelor suite in the downtown neighborhood of Oliver in the City of Edmonton. Her most memorable years were spent at the University of Alberta, where she graduated with Distinction with a degree in Anthropology (1975). She has lived successfully with schizophrenia for many years and is a member of the Writers' Guild of Alberta and the Canadian Authors Association. She has three wonderful children and three grandsons.

References

Her author's blog: http://www.KennaMcKinnonAuthor.com/
Facebook: https://www.facebook.com/KennaMcKinnonAuthor
Twitter: http://www.twitter.com/KennaMcKinnon
Goodreads: https://www.goodreads.com/author/show/6480104.Kenna_McKinnon
LinkedIn: http://www.linkedin.com/in/kennamckinnon
Google+: https://plus.google.com/118297240319245529549/posts

Made in the USA
Charleston, SC
24 May 2016